W9-BXU-598

On the far edge of the Phantom Waste,
the watchman at way station 727 retrieves a message.

Outbound Survey Ship, *Indomitable*, in tracking mode . . .

Sequence of events compiled by Wesley Singleton from available source material.

CLASSIFIED
3517—10.15. OFFICIAL REPORT OF AIR SERVICE
OFFICIAL TRANSCRIPT / GONDOLA VOICE RECORDER

12:42:34

> RUN PROGRAM

| | | | | | | | | |

October 15. 12:43:22 Solar

GALEN SINGLETON
Ping coordinates again, please, Mr. Edwards.

TOMISON EDWARDS
Aye. Pinging now.

CAPT. LATHOM
Helm, one-third speed. Prep for silent running.
Bring 'er sou'sou'west along the beam. Slipstream.

HELMSMAN
Aye, cavitation to 300rpm.

CAPT. LATHOM
Weatherman. Report.

WEATHERMAN
Winds out north-northwest at ten knots. Twenty-mile front.
Barometer dropping rapidly.
Sir—we're in for some real chop against this one.

CAPT. LATHOM
Advise.

WEATHERMAN
Suggest we climb to 10,000. Let the storm roll under us, Cap'n.

EDWARDS
SNONAR here. Echo return—confirmed, Mr. Singleton. We have it!

SINGLETON
These are the best soundings in twenty-five days, Captain.
Signal strength excellent. Beyond the scope.

CAPT. LATHOM
Electrical?

WEATHERMAN
Strikes increasing, Captain. Critical level, twelve minutes.

SINGLETON
Request descent before the storm makes our position, Captain.

CAPT. LATHOM
Agreed. Helm, take her down. Descent one-third, fifteen degrees
down angle on the planes.

OARSMAN
Aye, fifteen degrees down angle.

CAPT. LATHOM
We might just make it—let's see if we can't anchor before it
hits, eh, Mr. Singleton?

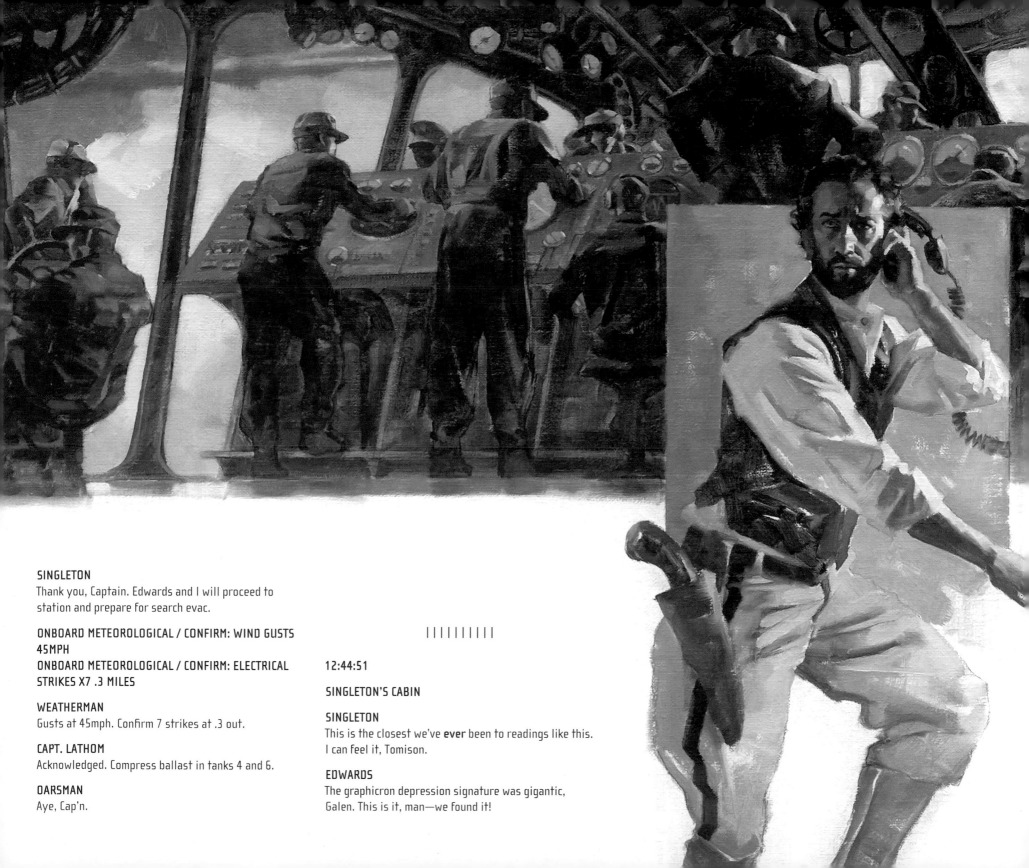

SINGLETON
Thank you, Captain. Edwards and I will proceed to
station and prepare for search evac.

**ONBOARD METEOROLOGICAL / CONFIRM: WIND GUSTS
45MPH**
**ONBOARD METEOROLOGICAL / CONFIRM: ELECTRICAL
STRIKES X7 .3 MILES**

WEATHERMAN
Gusts at 45mph. Confirm 7 strikes at .3 out.

CAPT. LATHOM
Acknowledged. Compress ballast in tanks 4 and 6.

OARSMAN
Aye, Cap'n.

| | | | | | | | | | |

12:44:51

SINGLETON'S CABIN

SINGLETON
This is the closest we've **ever** been to readings like this.
I can feel it, Tomison.

EDWARDS
The graphicron depression signature was gigantic,
Galen. This is it, man—we found it!

SINGLETON
If I know Lathom, he'll put up a fight. But then, that's why I hired him.

PROXIMITY MUNITIONS DETONATION X1

SINGLETON
Wait—that wasn't lightning . . .

> GENERAL INTERCOM
All hands to battle stations. All hands! Battle stations!

SINGLETON
Not again! Edwards, prep for evac. I've got to get topside, to the bubble.

EDWARDS
Galen, wait!

> VOICE STOP

| | | | | | | | | | |

12:45:21

> GENERAL INTERCOM
That first shot was not a greeting, Captain.

CAPT. LATHOM
This is a scientific research vessel! I am Captain Johansson. To whom am I addressing?

> GENERAL INTERCOM
Come now, Captain. There's no need for formalities out here. I'm the commander of the **ADAMANT**. You will heave to or I'll destroy your ship.

CAPT. LATHOM
Helm! Open hangar doors! Prep bi-wing release!

OARSMAN
Captain. We've lost rudder control, sir—she won't budge.

> GENERAL INTERCOM
This is Singleton, Captain—observation bubble.

CAPT. LATHOM
Report.

SINGLETON
They hit us from directly above. Stealth ship, rapid descent.

CAPT. LATHOM
Report to hangar deck, Mr. Singleton. You can slip away in the Mosquito. I'll deal with these cutthroats.

SINGLETON
No, Captain, I can help—

CAPT. LATHOM
Galen, you paid for my silence back home. Out here, my ship comes first.

SINGLETON
Sir! I won't leave y—

CAPT. LATHOM
I can best this thief and get the crew off! Get to the hangar deck! That's an order!

PROXIMITY MUNITIONS DETONATION X1

12:46:11

> GENERAL INTERCOM
Perhaps I hadn't made my point clear enough, Captain. I'm not waiting.

CAPT. LATHOM
Helm! Prepare for explosive decompression in tanks 5 through 12! Thirty degrees up angle on the planes! Fire deck—open starboard doors and bring tubes to bare, range two-hundred!

12:49:25

AIRMAN
Cap'n, stern crew.

LATHOM
Little busy here, Lieutenant.

AIRMAN
Fire in the tail section, sir. We sealed off the cells, but they're leaking gas like a stuck bleen fish. She's finished, Cap'n.

CAPT. LATHOM
Not if I can help it, Lieutenant.
Waist gunners! Set starboard guns to full pressure!

CAPT. LATHOM / GENERAL INTERCOM
All hands, hold on to your lunch!
Mr. Davers! Put us on the ceiling!

> **Aboard the ADAMANT.**

SCOPEMAN / ADAMANT
They're coming up at us, Commander!

COMMANDER / ADAMANT
What?!

SCOPEMAN / ADAMANT
Sixty feet per—they'll ram us in seven seconds, sir!

COMMANDER / ADAMANT
Starboard roll CRITICAL! Execute now! now! now!

> **Aboard the INDOMITABLE.**

CAPT. LATHOM
Gunners—FIRE!

INDOMITABLE / STARBOARD ROLL POSITIVE
HEAT SPIKE HOLLOW BAG-BREAKERS RELEASED X6

12:52:03

ADAMANT rolled away and the bag breakers overshot.

COMMANDER / ADAMANT
Port waist gunners! Target engines and fire!

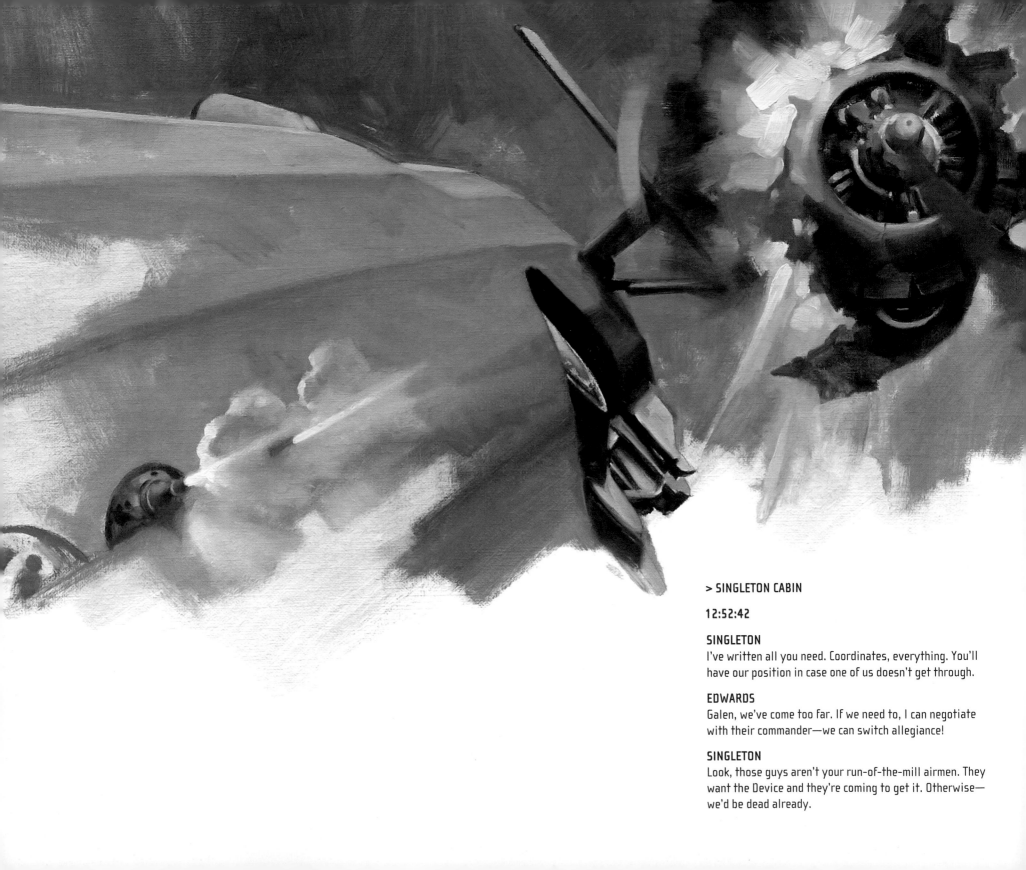

> SINGLETON CABIN

12:52:42

SINGLETON
I've written all you need. Coordinates, everything. You'll have our position in case one of us doesn't get through.

EDWARDS
Galen, we've come too far. If we need to, I can negotiate with their commander—we can switch allegiance!

SINGLETON
Look, those guys aren't your run-of-the-mill airmen. They want the Device and they're coming to get it. Otherwise—we'd be dead already.

> GENERAL INTERCOM / INDOMITABLE

CAPT. LATHOM
Ripper teams to forward gondola!
Gentlemen, we're about to be boarded. I'll keep 'er aloft as
long as possible.

> HULL CONTACT 12:54:01

CAPT. LATHOM
You are the finest crew any captain could be honored to
fly with.

IIIIIIIIII

12:54:31

VOICE STOP

IIIIIIIIII

EDWARDS
Then I'm gonna drop the Arktos Device out the tail deck with
a beacon.

SINGLETON
I didn't bring it! I wasn't about to risk losing it without
knowing the City's here!

EDWARDS
But we agreed you'd bring it!

SINGLETON
Tomison! The engines are on **fire**! There's a slight chance we
can escape from the hangar deck. Besides, I recognize that
commander's voice.

> ABOARD ADAMANT

COMMANDER / ADAMANT
They never believe me. Crewman, extend umbilical.

GALEN JOURNAL 3517

Edwards and I split up just in case. Had to take our chances in the Mosquito. I wanted to stay, help get the crew off. The least I could do was warn them on the way. It slowed me down but gave Edwards a chance to make it to the hangar deck.

> SHOTS FIRED X2

12:57:17

CREWMAN
Hold your fire! That's Mr. Singleton! Sorry, sir!

SINGLETON
How many are you?

CREWMAN
All of us, Mr. Singleton. The entire crew—what's left.

SINGLETON
We're not gonna win this one, gents. Get to the drop cables, and just before the hard deck, blow ballast for lift. If she's not on fire, we can **all** make it!

CREWMAN
(unintelligible) not leaving without a fight, sir. We can take 'em!

SINGLETON
You'll **have** to scatter rearward, then, that way—

CREWMAN
The boys are fighting the fire in the stern, sir. Not much point.

SINGLETON
Then . . . get a grappler crew up to starboard missile deck. You can use **ADAMANT**'s buoyancy for soft descent!

Don't let them release that umbilical!

AIRSHIP ADAMANT

13:01:19

COMMANDER / ADAMANT
Bi-wing pilot, meet me on the hangar deck. Prep for eject.
Bridge crew, release umbilical.

1ST OFFICER / ADAMANT
But, sir—our men on the **INDOMITABLE** will—

COMMANDER
She's on fire, fool! When that piece of junk goes down,
she'll pull us with it. Detach now! What we want, gentlemen,
will be on their escape wing.

PILOT / ADAMANT
It's madness to attempt to fly in this soup, sir.

COMMANDER / ADAMANT
Then you're welcome to a fine aerial discharge on our
return. Otherwise, set for wing release on my command.

> COCKPIT HATCH CLOSE

13:02:41

GALEN JOURNAL

I'd gotten to the hangar deck, but no sign of Edwards.
I heard shots fired from amidships.

GALEN JOURNAL

I'd hoped their pneumatics would run out, but it didn't matter. We were finished.

In the cockpit, I primed the booster. Heard the hatch open and told Edwards to grab a flight suit.

But it wasn't Edwards.

13:03:06

INDOMITABLE / HANGAR DECK

UNKNOWN VOICE
Freeze!

> SHOTS FIRED / AUTOMATIC WEAPONS

GALEN JOURNAL

I ducked down in the cockpit, pulled the release bar.
The Mosquito fell away.

I *hoped* the men would make it. At this range, the
grappler crew couldn't miss. They'd bury 'em deep.

And they risked their lives to save mine.

13:04:08

INDOMITABLE / LINER DECK /
GUN DECK SGT.
Fire, boys! FIRE!

> POWER-ASSIST GRAPPLER HOOK RELEASED X7

> VOICE STOP 13:04:13

| | | | | | | | | |

> TRANSCRIPT STOP
> END PROGRAM
> END PROGRAM

GALEN JOURNAL

I drop-kicked the Mosquito into a 5,000-foot suicide dive, with the engine on fire. Shots must've hit the feeder tubes.

There was no way to know how far I'd get, but I ran— a cowardly run from the carnage. They let me go, all those men, all my friends . . . their lives to save mine.

The signal flare won't attract much attention and the wireless has a clean hole through it. For all I know, someone will find my wreckage someday, my hand forever gripping the stick of the Staggerwing. What I deserve.

Out here.

Above the timberline.

GREGORY MANCHESS

ABOVE THE

T I M B E R L I N E

SAGA PRESS

LONDON SYDNEY NEW YORK TORONTO NEW DELHI

I've been steaming for three days.

They say ya gotta have talent to be an explorer. But the Air Service told me I didn't need any to be a pilot. So I joined up.

Only this isn't flying. Seems the more I resist the Waste, the more it pulls me back in.

Galen Singleton was lost this time. Seriously lost.

Not as if he hadn't gone missing on other expeditions, though somehow he always made it back. But this time doesn't look good.

Even for him.

Look him up, you get "World-class explorer for the Polaris Geographic Society, Discoverer of the Great Plateau." They should've added: "Absentee father. Searches for lost treasure under the ice." Had he searched close enough, he might've discovered he had a family.

It would've been easy to give up on him, but the note showed up.

AIRSHIP DOWN. RATIONS LOW.
NOWHERE.

WES JOURNAL 2 June, 3518

That's what forced my hand, and my only chance
to gain his respect. This whole thing, the whole
rescue effort, would be easier, if I hadn't learned
to hate him so much.

I'm Wesley Singleton, and I'm his son.

GALEN JOURNAL 13 December, 3517

Drilling again today. We penetrated to just over
500 feet. This area is rumored to hold trapped
air. Measured environmental shift in temperature,
atmospheric anomaly, pollution. Stretched
fifteen core samples across a one-mile spread.

Third year collecting. Samples generally show
global temps increased. Speculation: ozone
weakened enough to allow CO_2 dissipation into
space; pushed the planet into extreme ice age.

Pole Shift occurred in late 21st; Earth's
mantle spun faster than its crust, causing plates
to break loose and float above magma. Massive
tectonic shift; entire crust broken in whole
sections along fault lines. Northern tectonic
plates let go first, thrown outward toward
equator. Northern continents collided with
other continents flowing from the southern
hemisphere. Cities split apart, driven into each
other, pulverized each other.

Speculation: some areas undisturbed by the
pressure, possibly preserved beneath the ice.
But to what depth? How many mountain ranges,
newly created, hide city sections?

Using a 21c atlas to match flow patterns
in conjunction with core samples. I believe it's
possible to plot direction of the plates. PGS
geologists also mapping tectonic redistribution,
but wrong.

They're missing the point. The old equator
was thrown toward the old poles, and became
new equator. Poles became equator, equator
became new poles.

30 December

. . . ice cores non-conclusive. Await delivery of fresh drill head. Cargo ship will airdrop in two days. I fill my time researching antique manuscripts from Polaris Geographic, a companion volume found by former director in ancient library. I'd love to get my hands on more.

There have been sightings of a mountain city, deep in the Waste. It sits in an odd outcrop of mountains, just above a valley that is often covered by fog. The city is up-mountain, obscured by relentless clouds.

4 January 3518

Drill delayed.

Spoke to director and begged access to private library at main camp.

15 January

New drill section airdropped farther out. Hike to site, set up temp camp . . .

. . . told the men repeatedly to take a rifle with them, even in camp. Numerous reports from this territory of ice bear sightings.

Why Farrell hadn't brought the gun is still a mystery. Most thought he'd left the tent during the night for the supply sledge. Not entirely sure what for. I hadn't thought night watches necessary this far out.

This was a particularly cunning snow bear. Watched us build camp and had lain in wait, letting snow drift over it to disguise itself, like they do with the rhino when they cull one from the herd.

I should think that Farrell had no time to react or cry out. He'd been dragged far from camp. It knew we couldn't follow it back to a den hole.

We followed the bloody tracks in the morning until we lost them in the drifts.

27 March

Lost another crewman during the night, but Ersland got a shot off before it got away. The storm kept us from pursuing into the white. This morning we found the crewman frozen, the dead bear not far.

Posted watch round the dial.

TRA

Chronographer

VOL · 125

ETON LOST

INTREPID EXPLORER'S FINAL ASSAULT FOR CITY

M

He wasn't the man they portrayed in public. Not the father I knew, anyway.

The papers were wrong.

WES JOURNAL 6 June, 3518

They say the Waste is easy to get in, risky to get out. Fifteen hundred years of snow leaves terrain filled with snow stacks, and crevasses that appear out of nowhere.

The *Encounter* ate the miles, tore through terrain. Built with pulsed-wave compression, she responds like a hare, but it takes a pilot to fly her over the ice. It wasn't long before I was getting the wing of this monster, and getting a bit cocky about it.

Okay—too cocky. I near lost control avoiding an ice pillar and startled a herd of rhino just beyond it.

I oversteered again, rocked the whole rig up onto the opposite track. That really spooked them and they closed at full gallop on either fender.

I punched the servo-tank, but the rhinos gained on my right rear quarter panel. I stood on the pedal and gained enough steam to clear one beast's head.

But not the other one.

The crazy thing dipped its horn, drove it up into the rear track panel, bashed it in.

The tracker twisted through a field of ice chunks before catching air over a small dune. It landed hard, tipped sideways again, and a crate burst out of the side panel, tossing supplies across the ice.

I am so forged.

ONE WEEK AGO

WES JOURNAL 24 May, 3518

I'd left the Academy early, returned home to convince the PGS to send a rescue party. They're the only ones with the means for a multi-leveled mission, anyway. Can't imagine they wouldn't do it for one of their own.

GALEN JOURNAL 3517

. . . we volunteered to recover First Team from the edge of the Waste, 20 miles south of Crescent City. PGS backed the rescue effort. Four dog teams. I know the area from drilling core sites.

We don't expect to find survivors. Crevasse-laden territory. Will use opportunity to look for underground access to possible city artifact . . .

23 June

. . . have reached location of last signal from First Team. They were traversing a huge crevasse. Some scattered equipment. Other than that, no sign.

24 June

Shift in ice reveals steel I-beam, some masonry. Recovered one sledge from first team.

25 June

Confined to camp: storm-through. Reading Johansson's "Guide to the National Parks." Parks must've been outside major population areas. Old United States split down center along tectonic plate. Possibly separated along original Continental Divide to Gulf? The volcano in Yellowstone Nat'l Park was past due for eruption at the time.

. . . northeastern cities slammed together; quite promising for exposure of ancient territory; possible site of Lost City?

27 June

Encountered nomadic tribe. Friendly. Shared information; they've seen First Team. Dreadful news: confirmed that team is dead. We followed them to the last camp site. Recovered bodies.

Traded pleasantries and some equipment items in exchange for help, whereupon they gave information about artifacts nearby. Indicated more is available if we supply certain needed items: Medical supplies, favored tools.

I've established rapport with central tribe of the Waste, the Tukklan. (Some of my colleagues would use the derogatory term, snowdogs. Tukklan means "The People.") Made several encampments in near-Waste to learn their survival techniques, culture, some language twists. These are the guys we should be working with. Strong-willed survivors of the ice. Hands-on knowledge.

The Tukklan share legends around campfires. Last night, they spoke at length about a city of the mist. That the City comes and goes. Sometimes it shines on the face of a mountain with two faces, then disappears. When the mountain is revealed again, it's gone. They call it by many names: The Shrouded City. The Princess of the Sky.

Good news. Wilkes has un-iced the American Museum of Natural History. Will celebrate when we meet back at the Society. Am proud of his work, even though he feigns interest in mine. He still won't admit that we *both* suffered from scurvy in the Southern Assault. We were too far out. He ordered me on a transport home, but his condition was worse. He just wanted the claim and the glory. He would've died on the return if, after my return home, I hadn't sent backup.

WES JOURNAL

The Polaris Geographic Society.

I admired it as a child. These are the guys bent on rediscovering the lost technologies of the past scattered across the planet.

They left their mark on everything. Fundamental ice management, timber extraction, layered tectonic archeology, reciprocating snow sonar, the non-combustible rotating steam plant, on and on. In effect, they reinvented science.

And a bigger bunch of ice trolls I've never met.

Turns out, I'm not much of an animal guy. Sure,
I can handle my dog, Max, and that's about it.

Father's stories terrified me about the Waste.
Night strikers. Ghost cats. How vicious and
unpredictable they were. Are.

The lurking two-legged animals aren't much
safer. Treasure hunters pillaging anything from
the past. Gold scavengers, sociopaths, murderers.

Thieves. The lot of them.

WES JOURNAL

Speaking of thieves . . .

Iceship Captain Samson Barstow, an old friend of Father's. I never really trusted ol' Sam, not since the last time he and Father went on a run together and dragged me with them.

He was supposed to split his share, but it never even made it in the post to mother.

Then there were the dogs.

"Wes! Great frost, boy, I didn't know you'd be out of air camp yet! Heard the news about ol' Galen. Dreadful sorry, son."

"Lost contact. So I'm speaking with the Committee."

He pulled out a stool next to him. I could smell the grime of his clothes.

"An' if I know your old man, he's havin' a pipe with the snowdogs, swimmin' in a spring, complaining it's not hot enough!"

"I'm here to tell—to ask the Committee to mount a rescue."

The smile froze on his face.

"I guess I'm not keepin' up with telegraphs lately. What's he been gone, two weeks, a month? That's nothing to worry over with ol' Galen. You know that."

He ordered a drink. The bartender anticipated with his standard smoker. A Bombastic—steamed coffee, cinnamon, and liquor.

"Look, son. Your dad's probably just in a spot—can't get a message out."

"One thing Father is good at is communicating position, Sam. And we got that message—six months ago."

Sam took a long drag.

"Love to help, son, I really would, but, I—I'm due to ship out in three days and I really have to finish this duty."

"Of course, of course. Father would understand."

I got up from the stool.

"You've been there for him, I know. Like that time with the ice clipper. By the way, how're the dogs?"

"Now, wait, that was—"

I turned away, headed for the Committee room, stopped and turned back at the arch.

"Oh, one more thing. When that payment comes in? Post it directly to Mother, would ya? Thanks."

"Aw, son. Now, you kno—"

I passed under one of Father's expedition sledges mounted over the archway, out of earshot.

30 MINUTES LATER

Frustrated, I cut through the barroom on my way through the Great Hall and headed home. Far from the smell of antiquated men.

A voice called from behind a wingback chair, seated away from the main group of members.

"I heard about your father."

A figure got up and limped toward me.

"Wilkes—Braeburn Wilkes. I used to do field work, but gave it up after my leg— Well, he's one of the best explorers I know. I'm sorry to hear it. About your loss, I mean."

"Thanks, but there's no loss."

"You're here to talk them into a rescue?"

"Just came from the director's office."

"And?"

"And—they refused. They don't think that it's worth losing more men to save one."

"It—makes sense."

"Does it, now?"

"Look around you, son. These guys'd just as soon see your old man wiped off the map, erase his reputation."

"Well, I think they *owe* him. After all he's done for the Society? At least an attempt."

I couldn't believe I had to defend him now in front of these snakes.

"So—I can see that you're going after him."

"Can't very well leave him out there, now, can I? Doesn't sit well."

"Quite an undertaking."

"Are all you guys alike? I understand the risk. I just don't have— I have to go it alone."

Wilkes turned from the light, used his cane to get closer. Scar tissue ran along one side of his jaw, under his collar.

"I'm a bit of an investor, of sorts. I'd be willing to help, but I'm not certain you'd make it. You're fit and young enough, but still . . . you don't even know where you're headed."

I settled my hat with attitude.

"Suit yourself. But I know exactly where I'm headed."

He let me get almost to the hall before he called out with another irritating question.

"I don't suppose you can tell me *how* you know that?"

"Dead reckoning."

"Oh, yes. I heard the note had the wrong coordinates."

"They're *always* wrong."

He looked at me funny. But I wasn't about to explain.

"Now, if you'll excuse me, sir, I have to go find someone who gives a spit."

"I can back you . . . on one condition."

"I don't need conditions; I need equipment, rations. The rest I do myself. I'm the son of Galen Singleton. I don't need charity. I need confirmation."

"Listen, son. If I'm to back a single man on a single mission, I need a guarantee. And we both know there's no guarantees in the White. If we do it your way, I need something in return. I'd be risking a substantial investment."

"And I'd be risking my life."

"Fair enough."

I turned it over in my head for a moment.

"So, what's your dang condition?"

"Let's be frank. I know what your father's after and it's nonsense. But the City itself—that's my condition."

"You want—the City?"

"I own whatever you find there. You get your father."

I didn't know if I'd find Father dead or alive. Doesn't matter. There's no evidence the City even exists, much less its mysteries.

"You can do this? I mean, you can supply me with what I need?"

"Son, this is what I do. No one gets left behind if we can help it, right? Finding your father is part of my duty to the Society."

This guy may want the glory, and give me what I need for the rescue, but if I find Father, I've lived up to my part of the agreement. He can have the rest.

"I'm in."

As I left, every explorer in that room was smiling.

"Good luck, kid. Yer gonna need it . . ."

"Same luck your old man had."

Several tables laughed.

They wanted to sink Father's legacy, bury it for good and all, every last one of those ice crows.

My failure as well.

SINGLETON RESIDENCE

"Mother! What happened? You all right?"
　"I don't . . ."
　"Who did this?"
　"Masked—didn't—see them."
　"Where's Max?"
　"Tried to stop him. He bit one . . . bad . . ."
　"Here, let's get you up. I'll call for the doctor."
　I got her into a chair, then heard a whimper from the map room.

　I found Max curled in a ball, covered in books and ransacked papers in the chart room. Nobody beats a man's mother. You beat his dog and you've doubled down.

NEXT DAY

I had the topo-map out and scanned the Waste with the dimensional glass. Not much relief, except for the Barrier, the one major feature of the Waste that pushes back when pushed. The sheer ice face that blocks entry to the Great Plateau. Every expedition. Only one person has penetrated it.

Galen Singleton.

I brought some tea. Mother stared at me.

"They refused you, didn't they."

"Why didn't you tell me?"

"You would've gone anyway."

"To flames with those ice trolls. I found support anyway."

"How? Who?"

"A guy, an investor by the name of Braeburn Wilkes."

Mother went quiet for a moment. Her classic resistant mode demanded my attention. Something bothered her.

"I know this man. This isn't good, Wes."

"Why?"

"Your father and he were good friends once. I don't know what happened, but Galen never spoke about him again. I don't like it, Wes. Why would he do that?"

"He gets . . . whatever Father found."

"You promised this? Suppose he's found the City!"

"I don't see a choice here, Mother. What in St. Carsdale's cold carcass can I do besides this? They want to destroy Father's reputation."

"They've *always* tried. They're all after the same glory."

"Father's last note, you know the signal. He's gotta be at the site. Look, I'll cover ground faster than he did. I can get outfitted in Darsuum, short-cut my way farther afield. Fast out, straight back. That way, I stand a chance."

"Not much of a chance. Wesley, you're seventeen."

"Mother! He wants to back me! With real equipment. I have to go. You *know* I have to go."

"These men—they don't play by rules, Wes. For that matter, neither did your father."

Mother walked to a small desk in the corner of the library. She worked a lever, turned a geared crank until the clicking teeth settled with a loud clack. A small drawer slid out. Inside was a key. She brought the key to a section in the shelves, pulled one of the books away. Her hand slipped between the books, unlocked a hidden compartment.

"The men that broke in . . . they were searching for this."

"Your father hid it for ten years."

"The Arktos Device."

"Yes, from his precious City. He'd wanted it even before I met him. It started when he discovered this damned thing."

"Primeval! Looks complicated."

"It's from the site. In this business, information shared is information stolen. That's why his notes are folded to reveal his actual coordinates."

"Two and a half folds. I remember."

Her voice broke.

"—he wanted my approval but couldn't ask for it. It was all or nothing this time out. To fail at his limit, fail at his best."

I marveled at its intricacies; rubbed my hand over the subtle depressions on the covering.

"He told me that should he find the site, he'd send for it."

She smiled, then looked up at me.

"He never figured it would be you."

TWO DAYS LATER

Athena and Feathers, my agitated messenger raptors, took the rough jolts from loading. I thought to reprimand the porters, but they were paid to load, not to care.

"Wes, it's probably not worth telling you to look after yourself."

"No, Mother, it's not."

She frowned.

"—but I'd never think of leaving without hearing you say it."

A slow smile replaced her concern.

"Fail better, Wesley; fail better."

The Cruiser got me a thousand miles out, as far as Crescent City, where I offloaded my gear and caught a train to take me deeper in.

The Empire Flyer. A quad-rail super steamer, she'll reach the outer edges of the First Shelf where I'll transfer again at my third and final stage, a small outpost of miners at Darsuum. The same one Father used before heading into the White.

Lat. 39.073738 Long. -84.450912

THREE DAYS LATER
WES JOURNAL 1 June, 3518 Darsuum

Overnight here. After breakfast I'll head to
the rail shack and check for the stationmaster.
Have to secure a mechanic to help assemble the
SnowTracker supplied by Mr. Wilkes. It's an
ice-eating beast. It'll make faster progress across
the Waste.

   Got to get Athena and Feathers fed before
breakfast. Give them a flight.

2 June
In the morning, I made my way to the shack,
poked my head in. When my eyes adjusted from
bright snow, I saw Sam standing alongside the
SnowTracker.
   "Wha—what're you doing here?"
   "Me? What about you?"
   "I'm looking for a mechanic—"
   "Aw, helm. They said it was some young guy.
I had no idea it would be you."
   "Tell me you're not the mechanic."
   "Huh? Me? No, no. Struts here, he's your
mechanic."
   A grease-covered Struts slid from under the
Tracker and stood, dissected me with jaundiced
gaze. He spit, looked at Sam.
   "Yer kiddin', right?"
   "Now, Struts—"
   "Sam. For heatsakes, we cain't be sendin' a kid
out there. What's the matter with ya?"

He shook his head, wiped his face with the back of his hand. Left a trail of black oil across his cheek.

"He's got military training."

"Yeah? Another war-boy? You remember that last fella, Pennington? He finally made it back from the Waste."

"I wondered about him—where's he been?"

"In the morgue."

Sam's smile drooped.

"Again, how many of 'em we seen come back, Sam?"

"It ain't up to me, Struts. It's up to—"

I interrupted. "Me—I'm on a schedule here. When can I expect you birds to stop yackin'?"

Struts scratched his chin.

"Aw, pitch, if he's goin', he's goin'. Come over here, young fella. Some things I gotta show ya, ta keep yer assets from gettin' kilt."

Struts climbed back under the machine. Before I followed him, I glanced at Sam's pant leg. Ripped hole with a bandage underneath.

"Looks like that must've hurt."

"Huh? Oh . . . uh, I fell on some steps. Nasty cut."

Looked more like a nasty bite to me. I slid under the Tracker.

WES JOURNAL 3 June

I dressed in layers, sheathed the snow knife, grabbed maps, forced some breakfast down. I fed the raptors and prepared for their release, and headed over to the station shack, where I found Sam, Struts, and others milling about the machine. Sam slapped my shoulder.

"Looks like you're good to grind, Wes. What're ya gonna call it?"

"Call it?"

"Yeah, ya gotta christen it something. For good luck."

I thought for a second, spit on the grille.

"Encounter This."

Struts was in the cockpit, cranked the injector. The engine sputtered up, steamy and angry. Thick smell of oil and cigars. Sam got serious for a second and yelled over the noise.

"Listen, Wesley. Get as far as you can on the first steam-up. That should set you up for the long ride. Sleep early, up early."

"I got it, I got it."

I unstrapped the hoods from each bird, sent them aloft.

"Oh, do ya, now? Sounds like flyboy here is missing the point, wouldn't ya say, Struts?" Struts climbed down.

"This here's the 4640 D-Class SnowTracker, kid.

She's built for the long haul and can handle the grind. I've been out on those ice roads a stink-load more 'n you. Ya got spike ice, spinners 'n snowdogs . . . Strange things happen out there, know whadda mean?"

"Sorry, Struts. Just anxious."

"It messes with yer head!"

I settled into the cockpit.

"Keep your mo' up, camp clean. Where there's garbage, there's rhino."

"Rhino won't bother me."

"Yeah, but where there's rhino, there's ghost cats."

"Oh."

"Serious as a heart attack, son, ya gotta watch for 'em. Will ya—Wes?"

First time Struts used my name. I gave him a two-finger salute, taxied the Tracker onto fresh snow, revved the engine, looked back at Sam.

"Hey, Sam. When you and Father were out last time—"

"Yeah, son?"

"Whatdya do with the dogs?"

"Aw, now, Wesley, you—"

I dumped the clutch, spun the tracks, shot snow in a rooster tail. The Tracker glided out of the rail yard. Snow dripped off Sam's face, ice fell from his hair.

Sam brushed snow splatters from his waistcoat as he crossed the tracks to the hotel. He made it to the desk phone, gave it a crank.

"It's me. He just left."

WES JOURNAL 7 June

That was four days ago . . .

Half a hundred ways to die in the White. Half again as many words for snow but just one for "rhino."

They'd punctured the firebox and the afterburner kicked in. I put some leagues between them and me before I pulled the drag chute.

Waited until my heart settled down so I could see what I had left. The *Encounter* was finished. I'd have to build the backup Outrigger and hope to get farther afield.

Hard enough to maintain your sanity out here. Steam it to hell and back, but I hate the Phantom Waste.

THAT EVENING

The wireless made it. Cumbersome, but necessary.

I kept in touch with Wilkes' outfit to let them know my progress. That was the deal.

"Ice Station Two-Seven-Niner, this is Wes Singleton. Come in, over."

The static popped, then cleared.

"This is Two-Seven-Niner. Good to hear you, Wesley. Conditions?"

"Nominal. Kinda chilly."

"Progress?"

"The Tracker works perfectly."

A little embarrassed about the Tracker, I relayed position, but as Father would do, I kept the real coordinates to myself. I switched to a private frequency.

"This is Wesley. Mother, you out there?"

The static stopped.

"Here, Wes. How'd you do? Over."

She had enough to worry about. No way I would add to that. I chattered away.

"I'm curious. How long did Father know Sam?"

"Sam? About fifteen years, I suppose. Saw him at the PGS when I first asked them for help."

"Did he say anything?"

"He told me he was heading for Glacier Country."

"I ran into him again in Darsuum."

"Darsuum? That's odd."

Static.

"Wes, you all right?"

"Sure. Talk to you tomorrow night, hmm?"

"Wes—I'm proud of you."

"Thanks, Mother. Out."

I fed the birds and thought about the next day. I didn't eat. One can stay alive without food for twenty-five days. Without water: three.

Lat. 44.179398 Long. -103.026047

WES JOURNAL 7 June, p.m.

I used both the static winch and supports to drag the mini-
engine out of the wreck. Finished building the sledge by
midmorning and started packing.

The sextant survived, compass, snow knife. Wireless
checked. Maps intact. My Winslow could be slung along
the rail of the sledge.

Half the rations were scattered on the ice behind me.
The sledge could only carry about a quarter of what was
left, anyway.

Deep in the Waste, I'll have plenty of time to ponder
Father's stamina, his will to persevere.

I had his journal out and cracked it open halfway
through. The title of a page caught my eye.

THE DEVICE.

GALEN JOURNAL

. . . I found a cavern for protection when I was separated
from the main party during a storm.

My life changed when I found the body. Poor sod
must've crawled in the cave, shot, trying to hide. Some
cutthroat wanted something he had. In one hand he
gripped a note. I broke his fingers back and read it.

Coordinates.

The other hand held fast to a shard of glass. Had
he tried to cut his wrist? No, on inspection, the glass
was fogged with grey tones. It was a broken piece of
photographic plate. I turned it over in the light, tried to
make out what it was.

Some kind of machinery.

GALEN JOURNAL

The City. Everything I'd read, researched, studied as a boy, everything my uncle had said, felt real again. It became possible again.

Those idiots at the PGS know better. If anyone can find the City, it should be me. Compared to the City, my previous discoveries were training missions.

The answers lie in the Waste.

Lat. 44.273870 Long. -110.551682

WES JOURNAL 12 June

Others had attempted this same route, turned back by the Barrier Wall. Explorers unable to find a pass-through before they exhausted supplies. Bodies lay as frozen warnings.

"I don't go into bear country."

I had asked Father once if he ever hunted bears.

"You might if you're starving, but no sane man would. Extremely silent. So stealthy you won't know they're there until they're on top of you."

Near the door of the tent, I started. Sets of prints. Broad, fresh.

Ice leopard.

Memory trigger from airship camp, survival class:
"One scout, many killers!"

I swallowed hard, swept the torch around camp. The tracks circled the shelter several times and then led straight out. I lifted the beam, scanned it back and forth.

They're waiting.

GALEN JOURNAL

. . . independent expedition to the southern Waste. Have found several interesting artifacts that I believe are significant, though this location is too low in altitude to be the City my uncle told me about.

A pattern is emerging that correlates to one of the old maps. There may be several cities that have collided, folded in on one another, that travel, like a vein of ore, through the ice layers. Awoke from more dreams of the planet in thaw; dripping structures, rushing rivers, fields of green. It lingers. . . .

Major find today: a rail station of Cincinnati. Uncovered ancient tile work in its rotunda-shaped hall. Apparently, the building was abandoned as a train station and used as a laboratory at some point.

Celebrated with my team and the Tukklan tonight. I believe these tribes know more cities strewn throughout the Waste. They've memorized places for access. Do they recognize a pattern? Have they memorized city sites?

. . . Tukklan trade fine crafts, exquisite needlework, delicate materials. I'm interested in their survival clothing, made of natural rhino wool and layers of wind-breaking skins. They also show up with items from buried cities.

I've determined that some of them suffer from a mild form of scurvy. Most necessary nutrients come from game, as they are accomplished bear hunters.

Working on getting information from the Tukklan about passage through the Barrier. Have promised fresh fruit and other needs in exchange for information. They are visibly excited about this, arranged audience with chief. Would need clearance from PGS, but know they won't grant it.

I've decided to exchange with Tukklan out of my own coffers. Will need to pool interest from some friends' accounts. Appeal to Edwards, Reckers, Wilkes. Wilkes may be the most enthusiastic; trust his insight and confidence.

. . . can possibly use artifacts to track pattern of city debris. Some cities may have coalesced in a similar direction when the mantle caught up with core speed, 1,000 years AS.

The last tectonic plates to slow against mantle speed pushed up gigantic wall of ancient ice across ragged centerline of Frozen Waste. Tribal chief Solon Kai has promised to show me the Barrier Wall and the path they've used to cross for years. Oddly, he wants no payment.

During camp, in exchange for his knowledge of the Wall, I've shared the Device info with Kai, in hopes that he'll know something of its origin, perhaps help me find the City it came from. Kai, clearly moved at the sight of it, but now feigns interest. Shared location of caverns of deep green ice, where I found it. He is very familiar with the area.

Arrival at Barrier Wall. One continuous flowing shelf of hard ice. Ghastly.

Sheer cliffs along outer edge. No man, no expedition recorded as having penetrated beyond this monster. Passage is covered throughout the year; snow builds up across large, deep crevasse that breaches the wall.

Will need to cross Barrier, trust Kai to direct us to an access wall, a vertical crevasse known as "The Needles."

Kai identified mild depression in the wall after a sharp corner. If not pointed out, anyone would go by it without the slightest attention. I've taken readings for exact location; not sure if shelf may travel or shift location. Kai seems enthusiastic to show it to me.

Lat. 44.179398 Long. -117.011642

WES JOURNAL 15 June

I don't like the way the engine labors traversing rough ice
and snowsheets. The rear power plant pours out the heat, but
Struts warned against that comfort.

    I maintained a constant speed to avoid quick-snow. Barely
strong enough to support my passing, some bridges fell away
after. No returning in that direction.

    With the speed of a snow-sledge, I'll gain time, but it's
constant maintenance. Every moment in the White demands
maintenance. Fatigue factor. Rest is critical and tired men die.

So do machines.

REPORTING IN, DIRECTLY TO MR. WILKES.

"I've made the edge of the Barrier. How's the signal?
Over."

"Signal's clear. Good progress?"

"Nominal. Just thankful for the wireless at this stage."

"Equipment?"

"Steams well. I think I can make it through
tomorrow."

"No one's ever attempted taking a SnowTracker
into that region, Wes. It's too heavy."

"No worries. I can take the sledge if I have to.
In fact, I may just take the sledge anyway."

"Yeah, better idea. Watch for ice bridges."

"Copy that. Make sure you bring the wireless.
Stand by for coordinates."

Why wouldn't *I bring the wireless?*

I gave him numbers, then signed off and clicked
over to Mother. I'll worry about telling her what
happened when I get home. If I get home.

19 June
The Barrier. They said it was big, but this—

Father found his preternatural skills here, solidifying his legend. Colleagues clouded by envy accused him of sorcery. He based his approach on a pilots' adage, not magic. It inspired my own quest to fly. "Never trade skill for luck."

I camped here for the night. Needed time to think this through. Maybe this was how it started for Father, another challenge on the long trek. An odd sensation crept through me—that he'd approve of the situation.

I was either headed back to deal with the leopard pack, or forward into Waste knows what.

GALEN JOURNAL 3517

PGS ignores info from these natives, thinking them beneath scientific methods. I've found them fierce but open-minded. They are respectful of a person's attempt at achieving goals. Spent long hours around campsite, listening to lore and mythology. Much of it based on actual incidents I remember from history, but their take on certain events is unique.

They put much trust in the "Native Eye": time spent in the Waste tests a person's perceptual abilities to calculate weather, game, ice conditions for survival. Experience highly respected. Natural talent shunned; more respect for work ethic. They believe the tribe is enhanced on the whole by dedicated training.

They are, however, pridefully territorial. They boldly defend right-to-land benefit. Nomadic. They have practical dimensional brain mapping developed from perceptive visual range. Uncanny. "Native Eye" indeed.

Hunters talk about the City. Tribal members go there but never return. It only becomes visible when it wants to devour honest men. That they cross over into the demon world, their cries heard by the ear of the sky . . .

April

Followed hunters into rhino herd. Couldn't keep up with runners. Sat out of way in snow dunes to observe.

May

Joined party for city scavenge. Could not determine origin of town, but buildings definitely Old European, PS. Ancient furniture, signage, technical papers in huge piles, illegible.

Following day. A section of Old Paris discovered. Light poles, ceramics, old coffee machine. More revealed but had to return to camp; will continue tomorrow. Talked with elders about this archeological find and its worth to PGS. They would pay handsomely to exploit this area.

June

Passage to Plateau: have made extensive drawings of the area; sketched features, traced route on map based on position readings. Very fragile snow buildup along crevasse ridge above Needles. Any loud sound, even a sharp shout, could produce the right vibration to disturb snow fields, ice bridges, or snow domes at back end of the crevasse.

NOTE: Avalanche risk. NO MACHINES THROUGH HERE.

July

Talks break down between tribes and PGS. Irritating. Those fools back in Empress City neglect the real value of maintaining camaraderie with native people. I've been given orders to return, no promises, no agreements.

I'm just getting to understand these people, just building their trust.

Late July

Night before leaving, during evening meal, Solon Kai shares that many cities twisted together, so much so, one can travel under the ice from one city to another.

He confirms that the "City in the Clouds" is a real place, somewhere at the top of a mountain. Contains a tunnel between this world and the next. This part of the legend matches the manuscript and Uncle's stories, but details are still unclear.

Will catch transport at Crescent City tomorrow.

August

Lost on return trip from Waste. Never made C City. Tukklan guide vanished in middle of night, left me stranded, waiting out storm. I think he overestimated my abilities, wanted to head back before storm. He must've figured I was fine.

Walked for one day. A spinner forced me to dig in. While constructing my tomb, I found a crevasse that opened into the most beautiful ice caverns I'd ever witnessed. Light poured through ceiling, changing the caverns to transparent emerald green.

It was here I discovered the Device.

Lat. 44.179398 Long. -117.011642

WES JOURNAL 20 June, a.m.

Tossed all night, visions of a warm Earth. Miles of gentle green.

I started the burn-up on the sledge early. Sat for a minute, let the steamer afterburn a little, primed to make the climb. I couldn't afford to get stranded on the slope.

Father knew the People of the Waste and listened to them. They knew a small pathway through. A place called the Needles. I suppose he traded his skill for luck, anyway.

I watched Athena and Feathers circle above the Barrier. Heck, they don't care. They're already over it.

That's when it hit me.

This part isn't about Father. It's about me. All I ever wanted was to impress him, to be a part of the men in his life he admired so much.

Scribbled in the margin of Father's notebook, and again on his map: *Point of no return*.

All or nothing.

I suddenly realized I don't know what the frack ice I'm talking about.

Yeah, I had coordinates for the passage. Lotta good that would do. It's not finding the Needles that's the problem. . . .

. . . it's having the guts to climb.

No wonder I joined the Air Service.

Top burn for more than two hours already. Can't allow the engine to stop completely or I'd risk a seize-up.

The steam plant ran at maximum. Loud. Sharp back-steam on the way up echoed through the valley.

I crested a small ridge and slowed for another rest. I stood forward on the idling sledge to glass the valley, scan the snow left to cross, study a snow awning. It reminded me of—

The steamer labored, fought for an idle, backfired. The propeller wound down. The engine quit with a final bang that echoed upslope.

I snapped a look at the overhang.

We used to drive these rigs all over at the Academy. I used a trick I'd learned during our late-night romps: primed the burn pan and fired propellant into the steam-hold.

Nothing.

I worked in a panic, had a glove off, burned my hand twice when I tried to open the flush panel. The ground trembled, shook the machine, threatened to rock it off the ridge. The whole rig slid sideways five feet and I leaped away to avoid getting pinned.

I glanced at the wall of glide-snow as it widened out and rushed down behind me. It would overtake my ridge soon.

I had to get enough pressure into the reserve valve or I was finished. I rammed the hose into the main chamber, leaped behind the machine, and with my whole body, yanked the slack out of the propeller.

I could see the wall of snow hit the base of my ridge and fly upward. I forced residual steam into the piston tank, charged the burner, and jumped to the seat. The prop kicked twice, burst into speed.

I had to force a restart after all.
I dumped the clutch. . . .

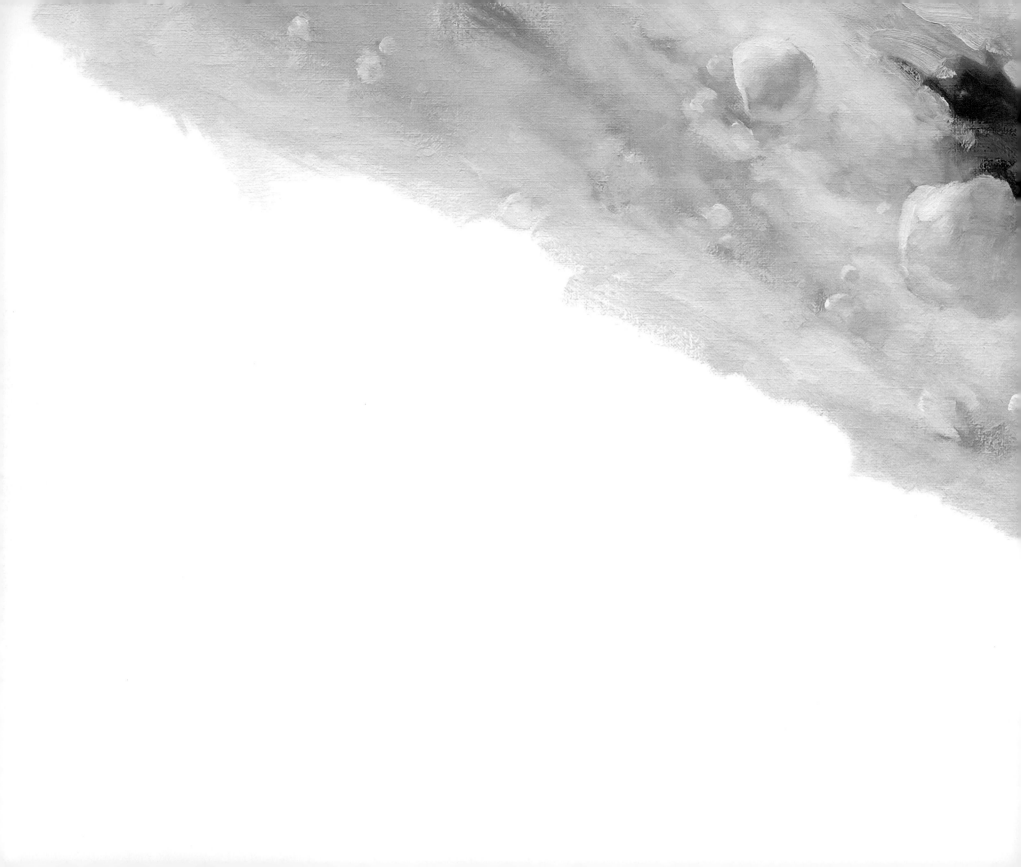

I missed the worst of the avalanche's brutal front edge and came down angled at forty-five degrees. I drove the edge of the sledge into the slide, maintained an angle of attack on the snow in a hot-frost zigzag to the top.

I crested the ridge and flew over the edge, onto the Plateau.
Have to remember to read farther into each journal section.
On the page of Father's Barrier notations in his journal:

NOTE: Avalanche risk. *NO MACHINES THROUGH HERE.*

———————————

ONE DAY LATER

Lat. 45.481463 Long. -122.815170

I have to stop staring at the map. Sunburned retinas can cause
continual tears, stinging pain, and make seeing an agonizing chore.
I called in the coordinates, then switched over to Mother's
frequency.
"Mother, this is Wesley. Over."
"I'm here, son. Copy."

"Who did Sam work for when he and Father quit?"
"I don't remember offhand, Wes. I think—Janice something."
"I've been reading through Father's journal. As far as I've read,
a friend of Father's was selling arms to the people of the Waste."
"He never shared that with me. He kept me out of the specifics."
"It's Wilkes!"
She went silent for a moment, then spoke.
"Wes, are you scrambling your position reports?"
"Yes, no info that isn't ciphered. But he can't find me out here,
anyway."
"Oh, yes, he can, Wes. He's got the means and the intention."
"I'm following protocol. What can I do?"
"Gradually increase off-course coordinates. Wesley, you must . . .
disappear."

GALEN JOURNAL

Have traded with a tribesman for a small curiosity. A stone talisman in the shape of a primitive bear, like something that might be from a wall relief or a shrine. Beautifully carved in white stone. He couldn't tell me how he got it, or where it had come from. Legend said to have come from a secret city in the sky.

November 3516
Back with Tukklan. Brought steam sledge full of fresh fruit, vegetables, some dry goods, tools. Came alone. Many at PGS now believe them simpletons, and refuse to cooperate.

It is a pleasure to work with them again. Their knowledge of the Waste is vast. Learned of distant barrier that separates our position from the "Cloud City." Impenetrable. But I believe they have a passage through it.

December
Interesting legend about a split city in distant Waste. A possible access site for tribesmen to travel along commingled debris from city to city! Shelf forced up by pressure fracture; an entry exposed in side of an ice wall. Suspicious of this story, though. May be misleading, but if true, may be important discoveries to be made.

. . . seems the unmitigated nature of the Ultraverse to flow toward entropy. All systems tend to break down; why wouldn't the grand experiment of nature follow the same direction, eventually fall apart?

That is why other explorers fail. The idea of rebuilding, of rejuvenation, of rebirth does not occur to them. If something seems impossible, then it *is* impossible. They don't understand it's not the failure but the recovery that matters.

Tribes know far more than I first suspected about the Waste. Is it any wonder: they've survived in the Waste for 1,500 years or so.

Nothing, no legend compares to my uncle's tales, however. City in the Clouds may contain technologies beyond our comprehension.

Solstice Festival
I've written to Elizabeth, sent short note via crow. Sent longer letter with scouting party I ran into returning from the Waste. They should make Darsuum within the week. Wish I had sent it before the holiday. Will have to make it up to her as always.

. . . The following late October 3517
Wilkes, on separate mission to southern Waste, refuses to replenish tribesmen with promised goods. I have put together a small party to appease Solon Kai until such time as we can deliver substantial shipment via airship.

(Kai could never get my name right, I suspect on purpose. Chose to call me "White Eyes" instead. I don't think it was a compliment.)

Intercepted scouting tribe 20 miles past outpost at Ice Station 279. I stopped one Tukklan who carried an old, pre-Shift rifle, asked where he found it. He was indignant. After near blows and some apologies, managed to have story relayed.

Apparently, Wilkes has been allowing Tukklan to keep weapon finds, but limiting them to old tech. This is why he's been able to make such quick discoveries: the tribesmen are hungry for more advanced weapons tech.

My old friend is dealing in the arms trade.

Lat. 45.914999 Long. -124.578476

WES JOURNAL 23 June

Two more days of steaming and I was quite far from
the coordinates I radioed in each night.

Father had written about entropy. The nature of the
Ultraverse to break down—something like that. He
thought other expeditions failed for lack of discipline.

No matter how disciplined I had become, in the
Academy training, or the Air Service, none of it
compared to Galen Singleton's focus. Or guile.

It hadn't been so long after crossing the Barrier
that Father's messages had stopped.

I wondered if he was still alive.

TWO NIGHTS LATER

Lat. 44.022595 Long. -129.472885

25 June
"Mother, I made the Plateau."
   The voice that answered was a deep male tone, and clear. Braeburn Wilkes.
   "You are entirely off course, Mr. Singleton."
   "Wh—what are you—? Where's Mother?"
   "I'm here to see that you hold up your end of the bargain, son."
   "I'm sending you coordinates; what else do you want?"

"You are sending false coordinates, and one or both of you know how to decode them."

"It protects us *both*, Mr. Wilkes. There could be others listening!"

"Certainly could be. So, here's the plan now. My associates will stay here and make certain no harm comes to your lovely mother, unless you send me inaccurate information. You copy?"

"You frigid—if you so much as touch her, Mr. Wilkes, I—"

"You've no idea who you're dealing with, Singleton."

"Next time I see you—"

The signal cracked, hissed.

"Wilkes?"

Then silence.

"WILKES!"

It hit me like an ice strike. They didn't know how to find *me*. But they *did* know how to find the *wireless*.

I ripped the plug out, threw the stupid thing down, smashed it open. They're triangulating the wireless signal somehow.

Sure as spike ice, there was a beacon inside.

Lat. 32.914353 Long. -137.031479

27 June

Trashing the radio was not my best move, but there was no choice.

Forced to rely on the birds now. Mother would be glad to know I'd made it onto the Great Plateau. So I included that I loved her. Sometimes, mothers just need the mention.

I'd like to think Wilkes is bluffing just to get me to toe the line. That bustard must've sent those men to Mother's in the first place.

I signaled Feathers with a sharp whistle: he had a long flight ahead.

Athena called from overhead. I pulled the glasses, slapped a filter over the lens.

Tribesmen.

Twenty-five ice cutters came about to face the Outrigger in a wide semicircle. When they got within seventy-five yards, a shot ricocheted off the fan housing, spun away. I threw in the clutch, turned hard over, and came to a gliding sideways stop.

There's too many of them.

I suppressed the urge to turn tail. These guys are legendary shots. I throttled back and let the Outrigger wind down.

"What are you doing out here?"

"I—I'm with an expedition and lost them in the last storm-through."

He stared at the Outrigger, then back to me. I had my hand on the Winslow in the side mount.

"You carry too much."

The rider climbed off the cutter saddle, pulled his goggles up, his face mask down as he approached.

"I am Solon Kai. I lead my tribe over the Span of Ice for the good of all."

"I'm—Wesley Singleton. I—explore."

It's him. The Tukklan leader Father wrote about in his journal.

"What do you search for, *Wesily Singlington?*"

"It's Singlet— Never mind. I'm— We're looking for a city out here."

"There are no cities in the White. Just Tukklan."

Solon Kai circled his weapon in the air, and the caravan of cutters surrounded the Outrigger. I got some food out as an offering instead.

"Share some roughcake?"

Solon Kai tapped my rifle with his own.

"You are armed."

I looked up at the circle of riders; each held a weapon at the ready.

"For game."

"This game you hunt—that would be Tukklan game, *Singlington*. And comes at a price."

"I understand. May I offer something for trade?"

Solon Kai pulled the Winslow from the mount, stared back at me, and held my gaze.

"The weak man finds strength in weaponry. I think you are but a boy."

Solon Kai climbed into his saddle and holstered my rifle in one fluid motion.

"Come, boy. You'll camp with us tonight and we'll decide why you are here."

Don't come down here, Athena. Just stay away.

I pretended to sip the vile brew they passed around. Just licking it from my lips made me nauseous.

"Tell us why you search for a city that doesn't exist, Boy *Singlington*."

"Why did you take my stuff? I've done nothing to you."

"All things are our property in the White. If you are telling the truth, we may allow you to keep them."

"Do you know of a legend about a city that touches 'the roof of the sky'?"

"They are tales. You read too much."

"But there's much written about it—maybe the stories are true?"

"My people have a tale of a forbidden city. Shrouded in clouds."

A tribesman groaned. I felt the tension in the tent. Solon Kai sipped slowly from his cup.

"Misguided men come out here needing the myth to be true."

"Okay, look. I'm searching for a man named Galen. You know him."

"So, you have lied about this city you search for. I don't know any man named 'Galen.'"

"Galen Singleton wrote about you. I know you must know him."

"So, you are his son?"

"Dressed much like myself. Tall man? Traveling alone. He was looking for a mountain city, yes?"

"I knew a man we call 'White Eyes.' We didn't use his name. You are his son?"

"You worked with him. How could you not—"

"I will not ask you again. Are you—"

"His *son*! Yes, for— I'm his SON!"

One of the more weathered men raised his voice.

"Why do you bother, Solon Kai? They are all the same."

"You *know* my father!"

The tribesman shouted at me.

"You and all of your machines descend on our pure land, and for what?"

I stood to face him. As I did, he backhanded me across the face. I went down in a heap.

"I'll tell you why. To plunder it!"

I got back to my feet. The tent spun, but I wouldn't let him see that. He kneed me in the stomach. Down again.

"Tell us—why would such a city be of value to you and not have more value to us? It is ___"

Solon Kai interrupted.

"Enough. Sit down, Mok."

The older Tukklan hesitated, then his legs folded beneath him as he sat.

"This 'City in the Clouds.' Devious men live there. They lie, like you. There is nothing there but trouble."

Solon Kai got up, stood over me.

"You are deep in the Waste, with no escape. Winter comes. Tomorrow, you go with us."

I tried to catch my breath from the pain.

"Find him a tent."

OUTSIDE THE MAIN TENT

"If he *is* his son, White Eyes would pay very well to get him back. The boy is in over his head."

"We can take what he brought, Solon Kai. His body will be enough for ransom."

"He's worth more alive, Mok. I need him. First light, we break camp."

"Why wait? We can—"

"Enough. Carry out."

I awoke, my cheek swollen and my back in pain. If I didn't find a way out of there, I was destined for a crevasse drop.

They'd missed my boot blade. I cut a slit in the back of the tent.

As I came around the side of the Outrigger, a tribesman rummaged through the compartment, pulling things out. I felt violated.

I tackled him into the snow, laced a punch to his temple. He dodged the stroke and took my feet out from under me.

Athena hit the back of his head. I jumped him, had him by the throat.

In the struggle, his hood came loose. I hesitated. Soft features, skin like shanna cloth reflected moonlight, eyes dark and gracious.

She whipped snow in my stunned face.

I shook it off, got my hand clamped over her mouth.

"If you cry out, I—"

She struck the back of my hand with her thumb knuckle. My hand let go involuntarily from the pain. She caught it, jammed my thumb against the socket, and held it. I stifled a cry into my sleeve. She had control, astonishing strength. She leaned forward and whispered.

"And if *you* cry out, I will leave you here."

I shook my head. She spoke again.

"Your machine would wake the dead, and you have no idea how to drive a cutter."

"I'm a pilot—fast learner."

"Not fast enough. They have—what you call them?—guns. On your feet, pilot."

I slid the snow knife into my harness, stuffed my pack with roughcake, grabbed the compass. Tempted to take some ammo, but without the Winslow . . .

She slipped from cutter to cutter and sliced the guidelines from the sails. That would give us time. She chose one for us, unfurled the sail. It whipped open with a snap, full of wind, and bucked against the anchor.

It was Solon Kai's. And I found my air gun left in the side mount.

A guard's head jerked in our direction.

I rolled into the cutter, heard the muffled crack of his rifle, heard the round crack the air by my head. She yanked the ground spike. A second shot zipped over us. Tribesmen poured from the tents.

"Where do you think you're taking us?"

"Away."

"I gathered that. Where's 'away'?"

"Far away."

Shots passed through the sail as she brought the cutter to glide speed. Athena beat hard to keep up.

"You always avoid straight questions?"

She glared at me, nearly knocked me out of the cutter when she shifted the boom. A shot spun off the rigging near my head.

"I avoid the rounds. Maybe you dodge better, pilot. I cannot sail between them."

We sailed flat out for two hours before she handed me the tiller. At that point, there were no ice stacks to watch for, only a barren plain ahead of us. She made it easy for me. The grating sound of the blades filled the silence, made it more obvious that we weren't talking.

Sometime later, I could feel the tiller wobble. My eye traced the sail lines hit by the rounds; they—

—the line snapped in my hand, the front blade buckled under and flipped us out of the cutter.

The earlier bruises were feeling lonely, anyway.

But then, there are worse fates than walking to "far away."

TUKKLAN CAMP

Meanwhile, Solon Kai prepared for a more important meeting, one that would provide his people with a greater element of risk but a far better payoff.

Before the Tukklan leader ascended the ramp, a runner intercepted him.

"Kai-Chan. Linea is missing. She was with the pilot."

Mok approached, confronting his leader.

"The pilot gets away. Why won't you pursue?"

"When the westerlies die down, we'll pick them up."

"We waste time. The Old Man might find them first!"

"I have my reasons, and your challenge does not go without reprise."

Braeburn Wilkes stepped into the hatchway of the Blackhawk M738 stealth ship.

"Solon Kai, Leader of the Twelve Tribes. We've lost the signal from Singleton's beacon."

"There's been a complication, Braeburn Wilkes."

"You planted the beacon as agreed, yes?"

"As agreed. Only, he left his machine behind and took a cutter without one."

"How do you suppose I follow him without a beacon?"

"I agreed to track him, not use your science tricks."

"And how do you plan to rectify this, Solon Kai?"

"Leave that to me. I want him for other purposes. Our agreement is sustained."

Wilkes stared at him; his voice pitch dropped.

"I need the Device and I need to know where he's *headed* with it. I remind you I'm paying you handsomely, or perhaps we should reevaluate our agreement."

GALEN JOURNAL September 3516

Latest discoveries have made me rather famous, sought after. They are not happy about this, but willing to fund more expeditions.

The Tukklan are gathering more artifacts. Before, it was mostly books, ceramics, furniture, and some paintings that survived and were the focus of tribesmen's finds.

Word came back through the Waste that some of their men had found the mountain with two faces. This visibly frightened some of the Tukklan at camp. They wouldn't talk any further about it. I don't quite understand— mountainsides face the points of the compass.

This piqued the PGS's interest in this new location, demanding more artifacts. Now pulling up automotive parts, machinery, electronics, and weapons. None of these work. But I'm worried they will reverse-engineer them in time. This will get dangerous.

October

. . . pulled a tractor from the ice, evidence that as late as 2000 years ago, Earth's population was farming. New evidence of warm Earth has PGS lab-men salivating for more. I call for funding at a moment's notice: A new excursion to the Waste with the use of an advanced airship.

With help from tribes to replenish stores, I can make it to the location of Cloud City for more prolonged search. At present, Society has no idea what this quest is focused on.

Now keeping all info to myself concerning possible location of the lost city. Will share with no one. Only misleading tactics.

November

Found more artifacts at previous site today. With help from Wilkes, who managed to procure heavy-lift ship, we happily emptied site of old machines and equipment for return to Society labs. Will need to bring Tukklan promised food stores and other necessaries on separate expedition.

Worse: a tribesman wanted me to explain to him the latest request from PGS for artifacts. Though he didn't understand the implications, I knew: Pneumatic weapon technology.

December

Received a message from PGS to cease trade with all tribal people, return to base, pulling funding. Something's wrong. I can't return at this point. Must find Solon Kai and try to use last bit of supplies to penetrate Barrier. This discovery will eclipse all others and make Kai undisputed leader of all twelve tribes. Hoping he'll help with my return home.

―――――――

"Why did you do that?!"
   "Me?! You hand me broken lines and blame it on me?"
   "You know nothing of cutters."

―――――――

30 June, 3518
We walked all night, crossed a timberline of breakstone pine. Fifteen hundred years old. The wood as dense as ice.
   The Winslow, now slung across my back, pulled and tugged over my bruised kidneys. My pace slowed to a meditative stride, watching my feet clump through the snow. I had to rest. My nose hairs froze from each in-breath, and my legs burned like pressure stokers. I can see the headlines:

EXTRA! EXPLORER'S SON LOST IN WASTE ON DESPERATE RESCUE MISSION.

   Brilliant.

Morning broke to the sound of our boots crunching.

This girl didn't talk much. We stopped and stretched, and grabbed the canteen for some water. One gets thirsty in the ice desert, so very thirsty.

I took a long draft from the canteen. When I brought my head down, I spotted them.

They were a hundred yards out and closing fast. The Tokklan looked perturbed and she mumbled.

"Typical. You brought them with you!"

"You blame it on *me*?"

"How else do you think they know we are here? They *smell* for a living!"

"You have a weapon?"

"Do I look like I have a weapon? I just have a snow knife."

"Then—circle up!"

I pulled the Winslow from its sheath, ram-charged the front chamber with the crank. That should get me thirty extra yards. I racked a round, and lowered the pipper on the lead beast, hoping to destroy their cohesiveness with one shot. But when the gun released, I missed him and hit the animal to its right.

One down, ten to go.

There's no way I'm dying in a snow hole, shredded by leopards.

Crack!

I'd overcompensated and drove the shot into the snow in front of the lead cat. It didn't even blink.

My trigger finger trembled. I waited, transfixed as the bright yellow-and-black eyes peered right through me. At twenty yards, I fired.

Crack!

Missed.

Too close now. This was gonna get messy. I detached the pistol from the Winslow, let the rifle fall, slid the snow knife out of the sheath. It was all over but the bleeding.

"They're gonna surround us! I hope you're good with that snow knife."
Big ol' smile on her face. She plucks my feathers, this one.

"C'MON! Whattaya got, y'bustards!"

I drop-twisted, fired the pistol upward. The leopard's claws shredded my collar, sliced my neck as the round tore through the cat's lung, came out through its spine. It fell away.

Another leaped. It was met in the air by a white wall of fur that smashed the cat, crushed its head. The cats screamed, snapped, and slashed.

Frantic, the leopards backed away, then ran. They looked over their shoulders now and again as they disappeared into the white.

"They're gone! We did it, girl! We—"

She wasn't moving.

It was crazy quiet but for the overheated Winslow hissing in the snow beneath me, and my thumping heart. A musky smell thick as incense pooled in the air.

Now I regretted skipping polar bear survival class at the Academy.

They rocked from leg to leg, argued over
which would dine on me first, I suppose.
Their roars unnerved me. Panic welled inside,
adrenaline flushed my veins, pumped my lungs.

I bolted.

Stumbled face-first, lost a glove; when I rolled
away to breathe, the big one pinned my snow knife.
I choked, tugged at my arm.

Spit, the snow burns.

It grunted at me, released its grip slightly.
"What are you waiting for?!"
It rushed me with an earsplitting roar.

My ears rang. When it sniffed my hand, I flinched. We stared at each other for a thick, dense minute. He looked to the girl, sniffed at her motionless body. She moaned. He looked back at me, growled again.

Make it quick.

Then he lumbered away.

Heads down, they prodded me toward the girl. When next to her, they backed off.

They want me to help her.

No visible wounds. Probably a slight concussion. I'd have to wake her every two hours, then. She needed rest and medical attention.

The lead bear started up the slope; the others waited for me to move. I sheathed the snow knife, grabbed my glove, and when I hoisted my new friend over my shoulder, they fell in line.

Now what?

We trekked awhile and I needed a break. I carried the girl to one of the bears, laid her across its broad back. They waited for me to rest, like they knew I was hurt, but impatient to move on.

LUMP

GRIM

PATCH

JACK

PAW

I'd noticed subtle differences in each bear. A limp, a scar, a mangled ear. Coloration. Gait. The larger scarred bear looked at me like, "C'mon, keep up."

"You don't have to look so grim all the time, y'know."

Grim.

"You either—*Lump.*"

Paw always pawed the air when he wanted attention from *Grim. Patch* had a spot on his snout, and *Jack* reminded me of a cat I had once.

Without the beacon, Wilkes was forced to track old style, though Solon Kai had had enough.
"This side-scanning from periscope depth is not working, Wilkes. We are losing time. I must get to the ice."

GALEN JOURNAL 3516

PGS has reduced funding for deep Waste search for lost city. Have decided to call in a few favors from the war to mount small team. Will rely on Tukklan for resupply posts.

Need dog team for assault. Contact Sam Barstow for this. Reminds me of the last time with Sam, when I brought Wesley with us. I wanted to challenge him, watch him develop. I just could never say the right words, or give the right impression, to his satisfaction.

The incident with Sam and Wes's favorite sled dog, Max, didn't help. Thought Wes should tough it out, learn to let go. I thought he would hurt less that way.

Max was the best. I took it out of Sam later. Docked his pay, cut him out of the payoff for that voyage. He was not happy and neither was I. Still, Barstow is the best sledman out there.

January 3517

Late nights buried in maps, volumes of past explorers, Shackleton, Amundsen. All class acts. But doubt they could deal with a planet in turmoil for centuries. What was once up is now down; what was equator is now pole, and vice versa.

I believe there's a reason the City is so far afield, and why the interest from the Society.

According to the journal of the man I pulled the Device from, J. Field, the City is more than I'd expected. He claims it possesses technology to cross vast distances and can pierce the fabric of time. The Device is a vital piece of something in the City, needed to engage the tech residing there.

And I think the Society wants it.

Field's journal bothered me, though. He was a lab-tech . . . worked for the Society.

Mid-January

I've promised much desired supplies, goods, and medicines for the Tukklan. I've refused trading any weapons, and admitted I had stalled any trades with Wilkes and PGS, which Solon Kai seemed fine with. He has enthusiastically agreed to show me the route through the Barrier Wall once again.

February

In critical survival mode. Haven't been able to spend time on log notes. Made assault up Needles as per Solon Kai's suggestion.

I was the last "barrier" to Kai's weapons procurement. He set me up for a speedy burial in the Needles. That way, the Tukklan could take their time digging my body out, find the Device, and use it as a bargaining chip with Wilkes and the PGS.

He just hadn't counted on my surviving the avalanche. His treachery killed half my team.

Losing light. Another storm blew in violent twists; I fell
backward into Grim. He had his nose to the wind, irritated
about something, had that look of survival.

"That's it! We're done!"

Grim snapped at me.

"We gotta get off this ridge *now* or we're dead, you
understand?! Stupid polar bear!"

Grim punched my stomach with his snout, slammed
me farther into the snow, roared in my face. The other
bears appeared out of the blinding flakes, surrounding us.

What do you want from me?!

The bears scooped huge pawfuls, dug for the harder
pack snow. They tore open a snow cave faster than I could
imagine.

My companion spoke feebly.

"My name—Linea."

"Wesley."

She barely heard my answer. She curled up with Lump
and Paw.

"The Old Man . . . will help you."

"What old man?"

"Pay attention . . . to your . . . elders, pilot."

She made a gesture with her hand, like a sign or an
emblem, then rolled away and fell back to sleep.

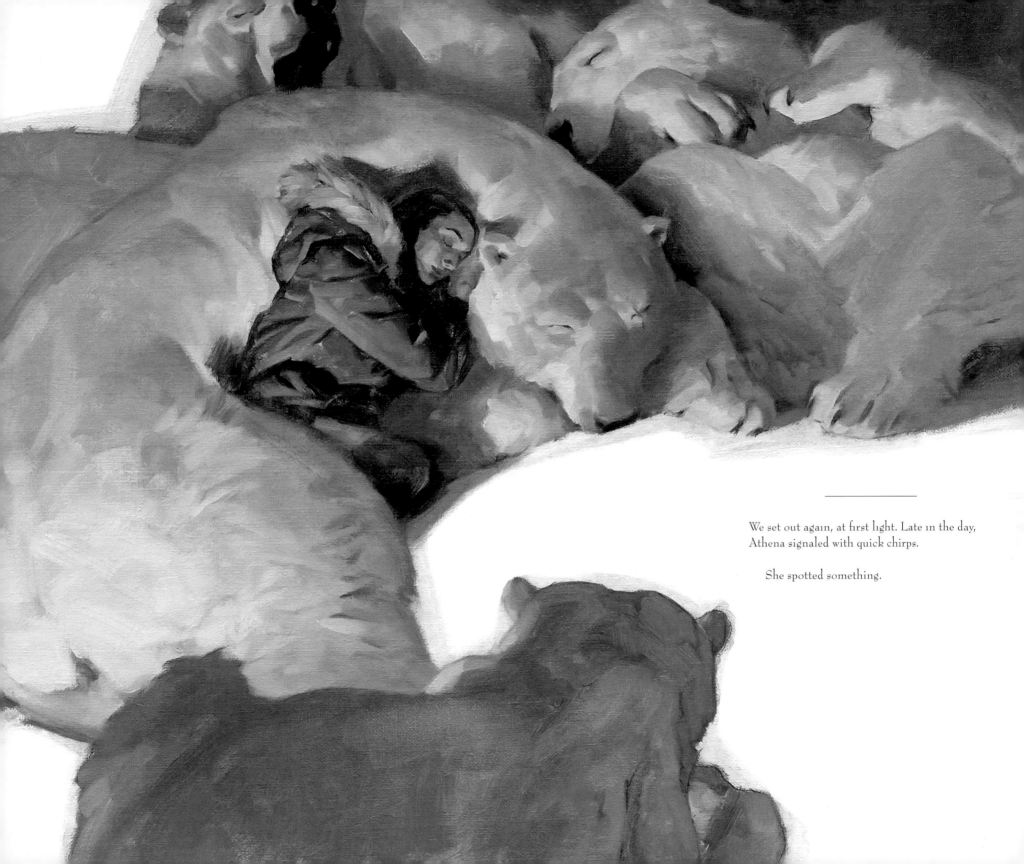

We set out again, at first light. Late in the day,
Athena signaled with quick chirps.

She spotted something.

We approached the gate at twilight, stopped by a sentry who bowed with a gesture to the white bears who encircled him.

"We are glad you have come."

"I had no choice. They brought me."

"I did not speak to you."

He noticed the girl laid across one of the bears, then studied me for a moment.

"Any weapons?"

"Do I look like I'm carry—"

"You can stay out here if you prefer to—"

"Snow knife—I just have a snow knife now."

Grim grunted, loud. The sentry looked at him, then back to me.

"Do not look so troubled. As always, the Old Man will decide."

ONE HOUR LATER

Another sentry led me through some passages. I caught the faint smell of cinnamon, pepper, and oil. When we came to the archway of a larger room, he pointed to a spot on the floor.

"I am Zhuan. Wait there."

"This is Shadow Moon Monastery. I am Tau. Why are you here?"

I stepped forward. Zhuan threw his arm out straight to stop me. His deep stare and head shake were a warning: no farther.

"I'm a pilot, on a search-and-rescue mission. The bears forced me here."

"After you harmed one of our own."

This is not going to be easy.

"No, no, I— We ran into some leopards and the bears—"

"Harmed you."

"No, sir, the leopards did, and the bears, well, they don't shoo away very easily . . ."

Nobody laughed.

"And what do you search for . . . pilot?"

"I'm looking for my father."

"What is your father doing out here?"

"He's lost— Well, he's in trouble."

"That makes two of you."

"He was on an expedition, and I'm trying to find him."

"What is your name?"

"Wesley Singleton, sir."

"Perhaps he *wants* to be out here, Mr. Singleton, since he is on expedition."

"Yes, he does want to be out here. He's—he's searching for something but got lost. So I came out—"

"And now you are lost too."

"Yes, but— I think I know where he is—"

"So, he is not lost."

"Oh, he's lost, but . . . I mean—"

Frustrated, I paused. Tau sighed.

"Neither of you seem very good at this . . . searching."

You can say that again.

The elder monk ended the conversation.

"We will see to Linea and have someone dress your wounds as well, Mr. Singleton. You are confined to the monastery village."

Tau was standing to leave when I interrupted.

"You must be—the old man."

Tau stared at me for a moment, then walked back the way he came.

I didn't sleep well. Angry monks and swirling clouds of multicolored birds circled just in front of me, swallowed me up as they churned, all drowned out by a ticking heartbeat.

I'd lost everything, and time as well.

2 July

Athena hunted on her own. Back in my room, she came to the window every so often. I whistled a patient note. She'd comply— for now.

Hard to tell how old this place is. The stones and artwork are highly developed. Repeating bear shapes—how many cities can be out here? I ran my hand over a sculptural relief of a bear image.

A voice from behind startled me.

"That is very old."

I turned and found a diminutive young woman, her eyes engaged.

July

Linea. She spoke again.

"Do you know this symbol?"

"Uh, how would I—"

"It is the Ice Bear. He took care of you."

I fumbled for an appropriate answer.

"Wait—shouldn't you be resting?"

"Clearly I am not, yes?"

"But your injuries—"

"Do not let the fashion fool you, Mr. Wesley; I am not that fragile."

She was native, she was lovely. And she'd lost all of her Tukklan gruffness.

"Those bears—they had me scared spitless. I thought for sure I was snack food."

"They have been a part of our life for a thousand years. Since the monastery began. You do not like bears?"

"I'd never been face to face or attacked by one. Like the leopards."

"They attacked you?"

"Who?"

"The bears."

"No, no. The leopards did. The bears forced me to carry you as far as I could. They carried you the rest of the way. Instinct, I guess."

She smiled.

"He's very mysterious. It is— His Way."

My eyes were transfixed on hers. She shifted her gaze away.

"You should be happy, Mr. Wesley. They eat the bad ones and throw the good ones back."

I must've looked shocked. She burst out laughing.

"Did you think us stuffy up here?"

Linea covered her smile. I relaxed.

Over several days, Linea shared the beauty of her beloved village. We spoke at length about our two worlds. And how to talk with bears, using your hands.

Twilight reflected from her dark eyes, and she caught me staring more than once. I looked away, embarrassed.

"I will come for you in the morning and show you some more bear signing."

"You trust me to find my way back?"

"You do not seem that dangerous. Are you— dangerous, Mr. Wesley?"

"I—"

"The elders do not know everything. Ancient knowledge is still—more ancient than knowledge."

She left me, grinning.

On the way back, I discovered a curious room, very old but recently used. Something in there, large, round, and mechanical. Why would monks have something so—mechanized? I tested the door.

Locked.

LINEA JOURNAL

I spent another day with the pilot from below. We spoke of instinct,
how it is hard to discern the difference between real insight and
imagined. How can we know that we *do not* know something?

I am still unsure of how the bears found us, but I cannot argue
with their natural timing. There must be something they detect in
Mr. Wes. They aren't as indifferent to him as they have been to others.

He is quite uncomfortable, inexperienced. His bear sign is
hysterical. Today he told a bear to jump in a bucket. It just walked
away. I think he thinks they're supposed to sign back.

Still, something different about him. His eyes are adorable.

Tau entered the room and set my pack on the bed.

"We are returning your kit. You'll forgive us sorting through it."

"Least you didn't beat me for it."

"Why would we beat—"

"Nothing. Just thinking the Waste is only empty on a map."

"They caught up to you."

"If you mean those ice-rats on cutters, then . . ."

"Respectfully, the Tukklan have cut out an existence only they can admire."

Tau sat across from me now.

"Why don't you tell me why you're really here?"

"I don't know that it matters anymore. I'm kinda reduced to this knapsack. I doubt I really need to *be* out here."

"You mentioned your father."

"The past few days have cleared my head a little. He's probably gone already."

"How can you be sure?"

"How can anyone be sure? Things disappear out here when the wind changes."

"Yet the wind continues."

Tau went to my pack, unbuttoned it, held the box out to me.

"This. This is more than camping gear or trinkets for natives. I wonder why a young man of your age is out here, far beyond his home, carrying this ancient mechanism that does nothing to help feed a man or even find a man."

"That's his, and I was hoping to bring it to him."

"This is *not* his. This belongs to no one. This is an artifact of the world, and only those who fulfill the prophecy can possess it."

"Then . . . it's yours. If it'll get me home any faster, keep it!"

Tau stared at me for the longest time.

"You have no idea what this is."

"I'll bite. What is it?"

"'It' is more than what it *is*."

Tau leaned in close.

"*It* is destiny."

I leaned right back to him.

"Might be your destiny, sir, but *my* destiny is on any airship heading east!"

Tau stood suddenly.

"You insolent, ignorant Out-Bounder."

"Tell me something I don't know—*old man*."

Tau turned and left the room.

I may have ruined my only chance to leave this hidey-hole.

LINEA JOURNAL

I am not sure how much to share with Mr. Wes. I am not sure
he trusts what I tell him about the monastery. He is curious
and city bred. The elders may be wrong, though. He bears a
Native Eye. He is as honestly clear-minded as anyone I have met.

Linea came by my room near the end of the day.

"The room you found. The elders are observant, Mr. Wesley. They watch you."

"I thought monks are supposed to be, y'know, peaceful and humble. Religious, right?"

She stared at me, quizzical.

"Monks? They are mountain ascetics, practitioners in the ancient art of Daijin."

"What?"

"Like the way of the bear, yes? You do not bother him, he does not bother you. Humble, yes. Still dangerous."

Linea looked away, to the surrounding mountains.

"These shadow mystics will protect their way of life from any stranger, any intruder."

"Like me."

I suppose showing up out of nowhere doesn't get you far around here. I'd ask her to convince them to help me, but she'd see through that.

Athena took flight, circled the village. I spoke across the awkward silence.

"My father used to tell me the ice desert only favors the tough and practical. There's no room for the humble."

"Here, the Daijin acolytes strike a balance. Their weapons may be old, but their skills are fresh and require a lifetime of focus."

Her eyes still didn't meet mine, but she continued.

"It is difficult training, learned from the Old Man. We have a saying: 'Struggle belies growth.'"

"This old man . . . who—"

There was a brief knock, then the door swung open. Zhuan.

"You will accompany me, pilot."

Linea's face changed when she saw Zhuan. She leaped up.

"Wait, Mr. Wesley."

She whispered close to me.

"If what you said is true, that you really are what you say you are, then—"

"Linea?"

"When the time comes—*do not fear!*"

VILLAGE: NIGHT

I was led to the town center, where the elders and villagers stood in a broad circle. They removed my jacket where I stood alone, shivering.

The aurora borealis swirled overhead, roiling through its spectral light. Tau spoke to the crowd.

"We are gathered this night to wrest wisdom from instinct."

Linea watched from the sidelines.

"Tonight, we uncover the truth that rests at the bottom of every soul, to reveal what lies beneath its frost-covered shell."

I watched the bears gather behind the elders.

"Wesley Singleton. Face away and kneel down. Keep still. Do *not* turn around."

This can't be good. I wasn't sure what to do. I sat back on my heels anyway. How do I get into this stuff?

"You have been brought here by mysteries that we ourselves cannot understand, yet we are bound to abide. Come!"

Tau signed the bears forward, inviting them into the center.

They circled and circled me. Growled and mock-charged. Minutes passed. Then at once, they stopped.

It got really quiet. The lanterns crackled.

Something was wrong.

Was the wind louder now? It became hard to stay still. My awareness skyrocketed, my mind filled the courtyard. I couldn't stay there. Something was very, horribly, crazy wrong.

I exploded to one side, rolled off my knees, spun to counter an attack.

Tau's sword flashed and smacked the ground where I'd sat not a moment before.

Tau lowered the sword and hand-signaled, and the elders parted at one end. Grim entered the circle of bears at full run, directly at me. *Do not fear.* I froze.

Tau shouted, eyes wild.

"You are hereby bound by the ancient laws! The Old Man decides!"

Grim snarled and spat, stared me down, so close I could feel his hot breath on my face. I shook, scared witless, but refused to move.

By the Fires of Franklin—he means the bears. . . .

"REVEAL!"

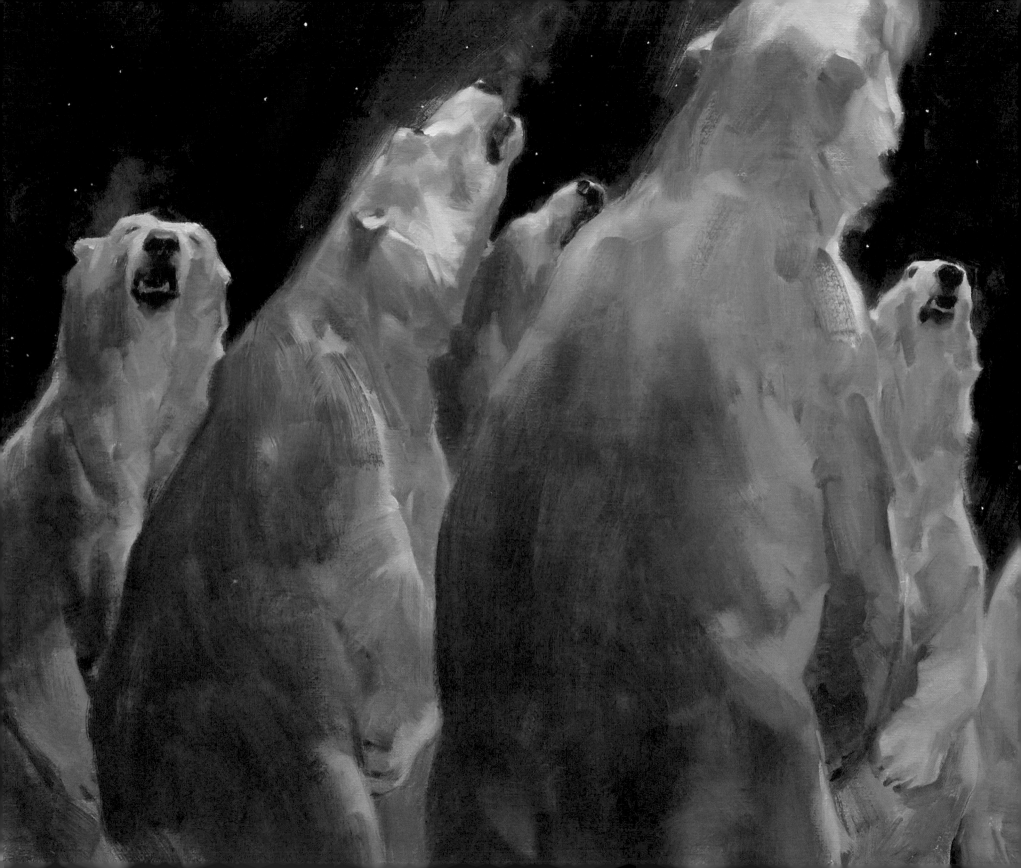

Grim stood teetering above me . . .
and began to howl.

The bears whimpered in unison, rocked
side to side. After some minutes, Tau's hand
signals broke their chorus. He strode forward
with a large coat. His voice now relaxed.

"Wesley Singleton . . . you have been encountered
by the Old Man of the Ice. He has witnessed you
and judged your worth. We do not know how this
mystery is unveiled, but it is our lifelong effort
to understand His Way. For this, we are allowed
into His World, as we at Shadow Moon Monastery
receive you now."

Tau wrapped the coat around my shoulders.
It was warm and quite heavy.

"Welcome, Friend Wesley."

Linea stood nearby, turning a nice shade of red.
She was happy. The elders bowed together, turned,
and walked away.

DAYBREAK, STELLAR CHARTROOM

"This machine looks like an armillary sphere."

"Star Catcher is a working star chart, a dimensional representation of the physical universe."

"Those are planets, then?"

"They are stars, relative to their magnitude, their size. At the moment, it is canted to reflect the Earth's axis, oriented toward the constellation Ursa Major."

I knew the seven-star pattern known as the Big Dipper but had forgotten about it being the Bear.

"Wait—you think the bears and the Device—"

"Are connected, yes. The artifact, lost for centuries, is now mysteriously making its way back to that city—through you."

"But—"

"I had to show the community last night what I already knew. That you are in fulfillment of prophecy."

"The sword—why?"

"A test of instinct, the Native Eye."

"Would you have . . . y'know—"

"I pushed as much violence toward you as I could. Had you moved any less swiftly, then . . . yes."

I didn't have the heart to tell him I'd had awareness training at the Academy.

Tau continued, looking at the model.

"It is said, 'The sky rolls over us, turned by the Clockwork of Heaven. It is not wound by mankind, nor doth he keep it.'

"We built Shadow Moon Monastery four hundred years ago. Its history has been distorted over the centuries, Mr. Singleton, passed down as sagas. Your father searches for the origin of one of these sagas."

"But what if Father missed it? Maybe the monastery *is* his Lost City."

Tau raised an eyebrow. He set a chair in front of me and held my gaze for a moment.

"Do you think your father is the first to come looking?"

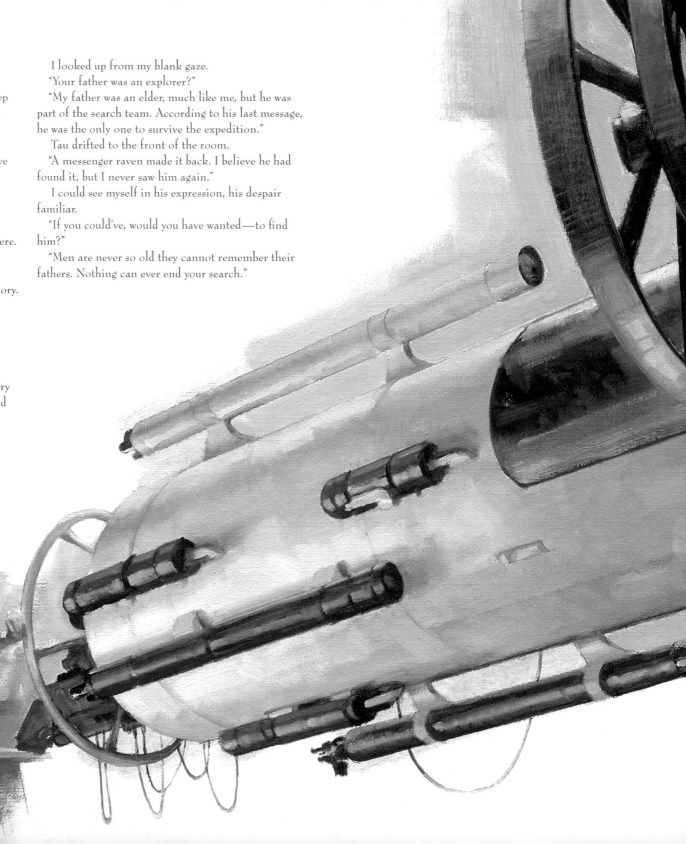

Tau sat forward.

"The ancestral texts speak of a passage hidden beneath an abandoned monastery—out there. Deep inside it, a mechanized door. Beyond that door lay the answers to the mysteries of the ages."

I looked at him. *That's just crazy.*

"We have searched for centuries. Yet we, too, have returned empty-handed, believing it is merely our monastery the Ancients referred to."

"Even *you* think the City is a myth."

"I did. Until I saw the mechanism you carry, Mr. Singleton. I know every path, every doorway here. Shadow Moon is not the place they seek."

"Then why keep looking?"

Tau looked away, then spoke as from a far memory.

"The quest is worth more than the find."

I studied the mountains across the valley.

"Yet my father *believed* the legend. That there's something *in* that mountain."

Tau stood.

"If I remember anything at all about being so very young, it is that no one could tell me anything I did not already know."

He grew quiet for a moment.

"I lost my father to the quest."

I looked up from my blank gaze.

"Your father was an explorer?"

"My father was an elder, much like me, but he was part of the search team. According to his last message, he was the only one to survive the expedition."

Tau drifted to the front of the room.

"A messenger raven made it back. I believe he had found it, but I never saw him again."

I could see myself in his expression, his despair familiar.

"If you could've, would you have wanted—to find him?"

"Men are never so old they cannot remember their fathers. Nothing can ever end your search."

There was something in the way he said that.

"You think you can find it, don't you."

"The chart is focused on a star that the nose of Ursa Major points to. And it matches the City's clandestine name."

Hold on a moment—

"Arcturus."

Tau put his hand on my shoulder.

"I do not know how you came by this Device . . . but I believe there is some reason you are here, Wesley. We only reveal the name to those we trust."

"I don't think I can take on the responsibility. Finding Father has been hard enough."

Tau gave the model a shove, watched it spin.

"Come, tell me what you know of your father's fabled city."

"I wish I knew where to start."

The stars realigned as they revolved about.

"When nothing is easy, everything is possible."

By the time Tau had shown me the location he suspected for the ancient city, droning airship engines and Zhuan suddenly filled the doorway.

"Master Tau! Tukklan! And they are—*tokai!*"

"Wesley, you must continue your search! Take the Device!"

"But, sir—I'm not sure—"

"Linea can lead you out of the monastery. There is a passage, a tunnel that leads out to the west ridge. She knows the way."

"But—"

"You will have the Old Man's protection. But you must hurry!"

Tau came mere steps away from me.

"Wesley. You are fulfilling a man's dream, from so many years ago. Your father's as well. You must make it to the mountain!"

Zhuan urged his leader.

"Master Tau. Solon Kai is *here!*"

"I would welcome you in, but you seem to think you belong here."

"I'm here for the boy. *Singleson*."

"He is not here. Left some time ago."

"That is not the story his tracks tell."

"The ice is full of deceit. You know this. He is gone. That is all."

"The way my wife, Dessa, left me—for you."

"She left of her own volition, Solon Kai. She wanted no part of you."

"You took advantage of her. She would've come back to me."

"Like all the other times? She wanted her freedom."

"You gave her nothing! I gave her a daughter!"

"And I raised that daughter as my own!"

The two had gotten within breathing distance of each other, then Solon Kai leaned back and pointed skyward.

"With a word, I could burn this place to cinders."

"Would you destroy her daughter's home as well?"

"It is *not* her home!"

"Then we find ourselves at an impasse yet again."

That night, Linea guided me through a series of
interlocking passageways deep into the monastery complex,
like an iceworm through masonry, before the tunnel
emptied onto a distant ridge.

"Where do all of these go?"

"The monastery is built on top of the original structure.
The tunnels are all over the place. The elders use them to
confuse intruders."

"How did you—"

"I used to tie a string to help me find my way back.
I memorized it."

"That must've been one monster ball of string."

We passed picture after picture painted along the walls.
In one particular depression was a sectioned image.

"Linea, wait. Right here. What is that? I've seen these
before, in museums, but this one's different."

"A bontakkla. Practitioners use it to train the mind to
be acute at visual memory."

"Usually they are religious representations. But there's
planets and stars on this one."

"Yes. It is a picture of the Ultraverse."

"Ah, but it's—it's *square*, not round."

"Of course. What makes you think the Ultraverse is
round?"

We made good time. We'll have perhaps a two-day advantage if everything goes well. But it won't be difficult to track five polar bears. Linea's face wore sunlight well. But I felt responsible for her being out there.

"Won't your folks be angry with you for leaving the monastery?"

She stared at me.

"Y'know . . . your parents?"

Linea looked away, looked down through the valley like she was looking through time. With a childlike quality, her voice repeated the story she was raised with.

"They were ambushed by tribesmen on a supply run to one of the neighboring villages. I am told my mother bundled me up against the cold. They missed finding me. When the tribe had left everyone for dead, a trader came upon the place. Heard me crying, I guess."

"That's terrible."

"The elders took me in. As you say, they are my 'folks.' Feels like running is in my blood."

She got quiet.

"Your turn, Mr. Wesley."

My turn to avoid her face, stare at the snow.

"Not much to tell, really."

"Not fair."

"Right. Sorry."

"Tell me about your father, then."

Where do I start?

"He's actually an archeologist—searching for a lost city that he studied all his life."

"And he thinks it is the monastery?"

"In his journals, he writes how old it is, how technological it is, something we can't comprehend. Buried beneath a mountain out—here. Deep enough to keep it hidden for centuries. He believes—Well, it's not important what he believes. What's the point?"

I looked down again.

"We lost contact. I came out to find—recover him."

LINEA JOURNAL

Something bothered me; felt like being watched.
    There was a time I, too, felt lost within
Shadow Moon Monastery.

"Perhaps we will find him."
    "One hungry bird, a snow knife, sighting staff,
the coat on my back. I've got nothing, Linea.
Nothing."

"The elders provide now, the Old Man later,
Mr. Wesley."
    "A pack of polar bears. Perfect. And look, it's
just Wes, okay? Call me just—Wes."
    "All right . . . JusWes."
    "No, no, not—"
    Her dark eyes penetrated mine as a smile
spread across her face.
    We stayed to either side of the tent. Linea
curled in Grim's warm hug. I rolled into my bag,
sealed from the world.
    In the morning, we started at sunrise.
Something wasn't right, but I couldn't put my
finger on it.

TWO DAYS LATER

"Look, speaking of lost, I'm curious—just why were you with the Tukklan that night? What were you doing out there?"

She frowned, looked away.

"There is more to it. Like you, I wanted to escape, get back home. You track?"

"Then I guess now you know how *I* feel."

"Oh? That what us natives do? Decipher life for you? Answer all your deep philosophical questions?"

"Hold on— I didn't mean—"

"Mean what—to come out here looking for an easy way home? Did not mean to risk our safety as well? What did you mean, pilot?"

"I didn't mean to be a problem! To you or anybody! Holy stinking ballast, I didn't mean to hurt you!"

We walked quiet for a long minute.

"My father's gone by now. I just want to get home."

Linea lowered her eyes on the trail, later spoke.

"That is because you are not done. Your heart is not finished."

LINEA JOURNAL

I cannot think straight around the pilot. Zhuan has asked
so many times to bind our hearts, and I wonder when we will.
But if it was not for the pilot, I would not have made it
back from the camps, to be with Zhuan. If it was not for
him, I would not have Zhuan.

He will leave soon, and Zhuan is there.

Though I wish he could stay. Crazy.

Lat. 46.558530 Long. -139.698700

Near the end of the day, we'd ascended another slope. If my estimates were right, we should be standing on top of the City. But nothing looked like a city. Lost or otherwise. Just another rock.

The sighting staff tracked repeatedly and the graph dropped to nothing. The needle wouldn't move and it was losing power. I looked over my shoulder, back along the slope. Ridge after ridge folded the landscape into a puzzle of rock and snow.

The rush of embarrassment flushed my face. I checked the numbers over and over again, but each reading was exactly the same.

Nothing.

Linea looked at me, incredulous. My face flushed red. At the top of this pitiful little mountain, there was nowhere else to go but down.

Grim growled.

"It's no use, Grim! There's nothing here!"

The wind ripped the map out of my hands, blown to oblivion. I slipped the journal into a pocket, but as I did, I lost balance in the wind.

The journal disappeared in the snow. I swept around, touched it once, but pushed it farther away.

I dropped the staff and thrashed about, skin burned from the snow. I dug in a panic, uncovered a crack in the ice, and caught a glimpse of it as it dropped farther down; heard it bang against metal.

Grim huffed, growled again.

"I know, Grim! The storm! But I gotta find—"

"He's not growling at you, Wesley!"

Frack ice, sergeant was right. They don't give up.
The bears charged up-mountain. The leopards
engaged. If they took the bears, we were dead.
Even deader if I lost Father's journal.

"GRIM!"

Snow fell away as I dug, a large gap growing
under the hole. The journal lay on metal
underneath.
A bi-wing cockpit.
Vicious, determined, the leopards backed the
bears downhill, close to my position.
We wouldn't have long. I needed a weapon,
something powerful, something—

The rear survival kit. Pulled the flare gun.
Linea threw the empty bow aside. She
hand-signaled the bears and yelled to me.

"Grab hold! We are leaving!"

I was on Lump's back, my hands buried deep in his luscious fur. Linea made it look easier than it was.

I yelled to her.

"You have some idea where we're going?"

"Does it matter?!"

The start of a crevasse lay ahead and Linea and Grim went for it.

She's crazy!

It ran laterally along the slope and just wide enough for us to fit. But for how long and how deep?

There'd be no going back the way we came. We'd have to follow this crevasse and hope for a way out.

The floor gradually became a shelf; over what, we couldn't tell in the dim light. It was instantly quiet. No sound of the leopards behind, but they'd certainly regroup to pursue us again.

Linea circled the bears around us. Alarms against the unknown.

We didn't talk much for a while. But my curiosity got the better of me.

"Why did you run that night? From what?"

"Expectations. My father says a woman in the Waste is merely prey."

"You seem like you can handle yourself."

"My father taught me how. He wanted me to be self-sufficient."

"Then he must've thought you capable enough."

"No. He wanted to use me to unite our people."

"A politician?"

"A wife. A political marriage. But I was not ready for that. I do not see myself that way. I *add* to the world by becoming whatever I want."

Linea looked at me with fired, dilated eyes.

"I have other passions, and I do not need to be dictated to."

"That's funny—"

Linea came closer.

"You find that funny, pilot?"

"Naw, just . . . I've often thought the same things."

She paused.

"The same. Like you, you mean. On your own?"

"Where I come from, you'd already be on your own."

We came closer.

"I want . . . that."

"You're already there. I mean *here*. I—"

I held Linea's gaze, close enough to touch now. But something prevented our kiss, something large, and wet, and black.

Linea wrapped her arms around Grim's huge head
and they nuzzled each other. Grim looked at me.

I got the message.

Lump came by my side and I rubbed his chin and
listened to him growl with pleasure.
Who needs the Air Service when you have bears?

DAYBREAK

Morning light revealed a harsh scene below us,
but we were right where we needed to be.

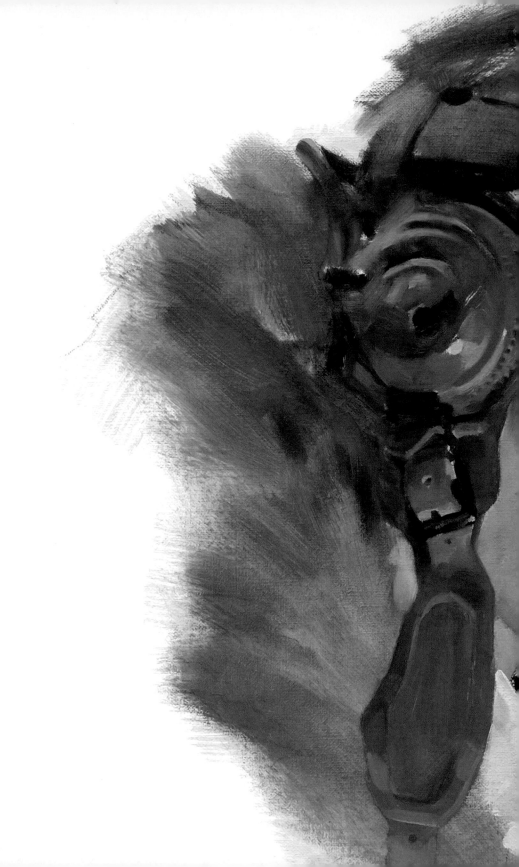

INDOMITABLE

By the time the bears had each found their
own way down through the crumpled strut work,
I finished a note to Mother.

OBJECTIVE ACQUIRED.
46.558530 / -135.698700
SAFE. FATHER NOWHERE.

Telling her about Grim and the others would be
pointless. They can debrief me later. I slid the
note into Athena's message tube.

*If anything happens, at least they'll be able to find
our bodies.*

I fed the great gyrfalcon the last of the meat.
Spoke aloud to Athena.

"You'll need this for the trip, girl. I just hope
you know to head home and not the monastery."

Athena shot me a curious look and flew off.
She was my last contact with home.

"Right. Let's find out what happened here."

INSIDE THE GONDOLA

From the communications module we could
access the bridge. I pried the bent outer hatch
wider and we squeezed through.

"Wes, where did you get that weapon back there?"

"There's a wrecked Staggerwing GB from
Indomitable up top. They always carry survival
gear onboard."

"But how do you know it is from the airship?"

"The insignia, on the kit."

"You think someone tried to find
this wreckage with it?"

"I know *someone* left *Indomitable* on that plane."

I was about to open the hatch when I realized
this was where most of the men may have taken
refuge at the last, surrounding their captain.

"Wait, Wes. Your father—"

"He could be up here. I know."

I steeled myself, swallowed hard, and pushed.

An eerie silence permeated the scene, like some
maniacal photographer had frozen everything in
time, a three-dimensional snapshot of the last
moments of the airship's life.

No bodies.

Dang peculiar. Most of the maps were missing,
too. No armatures, no penetrators or sounding
charts. Maybe the crew survived and tried to make
their way back. I noticed some of the first-aid and
survival kits were missing from the lockers.

In a corner of the gondola, several blankets were
curled in a jumble, like someone had just gotten up
from sleeping and left. The ship's charts were laid
in neat rows next to this nest-like little home.

"Maybe they—"

I rummaged through the blankets and boxes of
rations and uncovered a stiff volume that resisted
baring its secrets to the cold.

Journal of Galen Singleton, Last Survivor of
Indomitable.

The front half of this journal recorded soundings taken, depth and altimeter readings, weather conditions. Father made notes about the crew's temperament and attitude. Some speculative passages about where the City might lie and signs left above the timberlines of endless mountain ranges.

It wasn't until the last section of the journal that I found a fresh hand, less formal, and hastily written.

"My Love . . ."

No date, no time of day. Father's words addressed his wife as if he sat by a fireplace, holding a glass of wine.

I've made it back to the site of the wreckage. The fire and concussion must've been intense. None of the crew survived. Even my favorite among them, William. They were flash-frozen, still-motion, by the time I arrived. I spent the better part of two days lowering them into the crevasse. I hope it went quickly for dear Miss Nottingham. I swear I miss her pawing at my hand for strokes . . .

The bears rummaged around, all grunts and snorts, the entire wreckage an olfactory exploratorium for them. Any frozen food would still be as fresh as the day it fell into this unholy crack in the world.

Neatly folded into the journal and drawn on the back of one of the airship charts was a general layout of the City. As I unfolded it to study, a handwritten letter fell out.

TO ELIZABETH

As I read more of the journal, the wreckage fell silent. Too silent. I found my way back outside the gondola.

All were gone.

I followed the distant sounds of the bears echoing from a small tunnel. There was dim light coming from the end of it. I emerged from the tunnel like exiting the subtrain station back home.

The silence of the place appealed to me, broken only
by the crunch of ice underfoot or the huff of bear breath.
It breathed a cycle of contractions, must've melted and
refroze thousands of times, beating like a cold ice heart.

Linea stopped and studied the vast space.

"Wes—what is this place?"

It came to me then: the City wasn't *on* the mountain.

The city *is* the mountain.

"Arcturus."

I brought the letter with me. Father must've known he couldn't possibly post the letter home.

My Dearest Elizabeth,

I awoke today with the nagging feeling that I could spend the rest of my life here, piecing together information with regards to the City. The endless fascination is likely to be my end. The people that built this are at once familiar and more remarkable than I had imagined. . . .

. . . my entire life searching for this place, and all I can think of now is what I must've done to you. I hadn't meant it to be so costly. I understand that now. I thought I could push young Wesley into the limelight with my quests, not realizing he had his own interests. Honestly, he never showed much curiosity for my work. Perhaps for the best . . .

. . . This is my last entry. The best of me is so miserably poor, dear Elizabeth. I realize now, the drive to find the City became my answer for finding what most men search for more than anything else: a way to beat the fear of inadequacy. To become. Perhaps my love for you will redeem the poverty of the rest of me.

I want to walk into the Society and show those smug blowhards that I'm not just talk. To watch their smiles crack, their laughter wane. It's my suspicion that, somehow, the PGS knew about the City.

But exposing them would start the agony all over. No, I must try to return to you as I am now, fully awake. With you as my light.

I stared at the pages. The letters disappeared in a field of white as I watched myself from a distance, lost on the plateau, lost in thoughts of childhood.

Father's voice now gave clarity to just how much he didn't believe in me. It was as if he led me here on purpose, whispered to me on his silent trek.

I spotted a tunnel, then a spiral staircase leading down. Way down. Some kind of access shaft, like the ones throughout an airship, with a center slide pole.

"I'm going to check this out. It's similar to Father's description in the journal."

"If you do not return, pilot, I will rename the City after me."

The pole was cold, frost falling away from my grip. On the way down, the torchlight bounced off the walls.

No, not walls.

How deep can this go?

I must've dropped fifteen stories when the pole thawed, became sticky to my grip. I let go and dropped, hit the platform hard. I lay there a moment, studied the massive shaft, like staring at the drive wheels of a locomotive.

A light flashed in my eyes and blinded me before two hands grabbed my coat.

I pulled back, pushed him away. He practically growled at me.

"Who in Helclive's Hive are you?!"

"Father?"

"Wesley!"

"Father!"

I grabbed him by the collar and yanked him toward me.

"You're alive!"

"What are you doing here?!"

I doubled him with a punch to the stomach.

"*That's* for never being there!"

He coughed, straightened up to face me.

"Does your mother know . . . you're out here?"

"You worried her half sick at night! You lousy—"

I hit him again, and screamed all the way from childhood.

"Hey! That's *starting* to hurt!"

I swung, right for the kisser, but he dodged it and grabbed me from behind, put me in a hold, and yelled.

"The Squadron must've rinsed the respect out of you, too."

A loud bang on the metal platform startled us.

"Stop it! Both of you!"

"Who's this now?!"

"She's . . . We—"

"You can act like little boys later. We have more pressing things to think about."

I felt Father's arms surround me now, squeezing me in a big ol' bear hug.

"Wesley—son . . . you could've died out here."

"You're alive . . ."

"I couldn't live knowing that, Wes."

"You're alive. . . ."

I hugged him with all the years I had missed him.

We made our way silently back up the spiral stairs. The bears waited at the top. Grim snorted.

Father pulled his snow knife, stood between us.

"Back away, Wes—!"

I walked over and scratched Grim's chin.

"Wes! No!"

The bears came over to me.

"S'okay. Long story."

Father just stared.

BACK IN THE GONDOLA

Father was cautious, and I couldn't blame him. He'd only known bears as man-eaters in the Waste. Though Grim kept his distance, they treated Galen as if he were from the monastery. Maybe my attitude toward Father signaled something to them.

He finally broke the silence.

"It's quite old, y'know."

"What's old?"

"The City. Doesn't rust. All the working parts—"

"Well, look at us, sharing now."

"I'm *trying*, Wes, all right?!"

"Took you long enough."

One by one, the bears left the gondola.

"You're gonna have to explain that one, Wesley . . . the bears and—"

"This is Linea, Father. And it's rather—complicated."

"Pleased to meet you, miss."

Linea just nodded.

I watched the bears wander off outside, wondered how I got to this point in life. Although Father did try, didn't he?

I pulled the Device from my pack. My turn to make an attempt at talking.

"S'pose you'll be needing this."

"You brought it!"

Father's eyes lit up as he took the Device, mumbling a bit.

"So beautiful. It calibrates, not just longitude and latitude, but . . . depth. Feels astronomical. Like an attachment for a telescope."

There was something familiar reflected on the Device. A pattern, a design, from the monastery. Tau mentioned the bears and a connection with them.

Something about the Arktos Device.

Linea studied the Device while we spoke, then reminded me.

"Wes . . . the bontakkla I showed you? There are marks here, like on the painting."

I held the Device at an angle. The impressions caught the light in a familiar pattern.

Father took the Device and turned it over. The pattern became more obvious to me the more he looked at it.

"What are you saying, Linea?"

"It is inverted, but they look like the constellation Ursa Major."

I smiled at Linea and continued.

"The constellation of the bear. The snout points to a very bright star."

But it wasn't enough. I couldn't quite put a finger on it.

"Father, this place—it feels like a factory, more like something built here. Like airship factories."

"That cauldron we were in must use tremendous power, spin at phenomenal speeds, Wesley. The gearing, the velocity, but—why? What for?"

The only thing spinning was my head.

"Father. This isn't a city at all."

He stared at me, as if I'd touched something deep within him. Maybe within both of us.

"There's something about that pattern and that star. . . ."

Father got to his feet.

And then I had it.

"It's an engine. The whole place is an *engine*."

"Do you realize what you're saying?!"

"Ahem—"

"Oh, sorry, miss—"

"Quite all right; I am used to it."

"—what you're *both* saying? It must use that star as a guide, a homing target."

"For what?"

It was the most exciting thing in his life. I hadn't seen him smile for most of my childhood. His voice high, he gestured like a fascinated child.

"Wesley—son, the City, the *engine*, it's a kind of *portal*. A doorway that compresses space, squeezes it next to the destination."

"A portal—to where?"

"Wes, that star—is Arcturus."

After listening to Father, Linea spoke.

"Then—the saga *is* real . . ."

The bears stared through the gondola windows. Father stared at Grim as he spoke.

"It was built here, but they didn't stay."

"They? Who's 'they'?"

"That's what I *do* know—it's not ours."

I looked at him.

"Not human, Wes. Arcturus, the real Arcturus . . . is still out there. Still—hidden."

Father held the Device in his hands. He was again the distant, driven explorer from the old photographs. Only, now his face revealed the toll of his quest.

"I lost an entire crew of men for this. Trusted friends. I was determined to give them a proper burial. Maybe one day bring them home. I owe them that much."

Father stared out of the gondola, past the bears, his eyes trained on a memory.

"I'm gonna confront the jerk who killed those men."

"Then the papers *were* wrong. You *do* know who attacked your ship."

"Yeah, I know. I know his black heart. He was a trusted friend once. Braeburn Wilkes. He's dogged me for years."

My stomach flipped.

"I think about the look on his face when I return to claim the site as my own."

He turned to me, held my gaze.

"It's *our* discovery now."

Sadly, his discovery would now be the possession of Wilkes. And it was my fault.

"Father, there's something I need to explain. Wilkes is out here looking for us."

"What was that?"

"I said, I have to tell—"

"No. Quiet—listen . . ."

Now I could make it out.

"Airship!"

"The Device—Father, take it! I saw vents on the far slope. Use 'em for cover. When you see a chance, head down!"

Grim growled, pawed the air. The sound blocked his roar. I shouted to them above the buzzing propellers. Useless. Father resisted.

"No, Wes. Plenty of places to hide in here. Whoever it is needs to get back for the claim. It'll be safer with you."

I hand-signaled to the tunnel, and the bears formed up at the entrance. I turned back to Father.

"No—"

"Wes—I'll be fine. I'm very proud of you."

His words froze me to the spot.

Did he really mean that?

"I gotta tell you some—"

"GO!"

FLIGHT LEADER
"RELENTLESS, this is Flight Leader, I have movement west of the site. Three animals just below ridge. Came out of nowhere. Moving fast. Engage?"

RADIOMAN, RELENTLESS
"Copy, flight leader. Commander, they've made visual. Orders?"

COMMANDER WILKES
"Release Wolf teams."

Jack, Patch, and Paw went down the daylight side of the mountain, hoping to pull the Trackers' attention away from us while we raced down the opposite side.

Man, Lump was fast. As he charged down, I felt his rhythmic muscles skim through the powder like an ice badger through water.

But the momentum overcame him. The ice bear tumbled, threw me off, and sent plumes of snow skyward. I ran downhill and leaped to Lump's back; getting the clutch of this bear-riding.

The motion caught a spotter's attention scanning the snow fields.

FLIGHT LEADER
"Correction, **RELENTLESS**, more movement due **east** of the ridge, sir.
Downslope, in shadow, about a half mile out."

COMMANDER WILKES
"Slide?"

FLIGHT LEADER
"No, sir. Too sporadic. I'd say it's an animal."

COMMANDER WILKES
"Divert patrols and release remaining teams. Clever kid."

If we could get far enough into the timbers, we'd lose them in the thick.

The first pine tree zipped by as we sped into the thick forest.

"Careful, Lump! Watch it!"

The bears galloped just to either side of the trees, virtually disappeared from sight behind each one.

They're using them for cover.

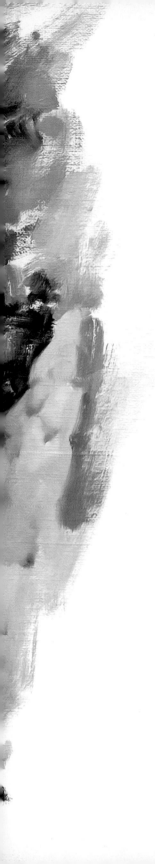

I could hear the Wolf teams growl their way toward us, but they had to be farther behind. Something else closed on us.

My heart slammed against my chest. I held fast to Lump's pack harness. I bounced and banged, but Linea rode Grim like a pro.

Wilkes' Mosquitos circled in and dove, one after the other, tried to drive us apart.

I know that trick, boys.

The woods emptied out, and they caught us in the open.

Maybe I was wrong. Maybe they didn't need to merely frighten us to stop.

Cold air whipped through my greatcoat, the Arktos Device slapped against the inside of the pack, like it might fly apart. I figured it made it this far over the centuries.

We lucked out. We covered the short gap between timberlines fast. We'd make the pines before they could circle back.

Primeval! I turned to cheer Linea on, but . . .

She wasn't there.

"LINEA!"

Lump spun and started back after her.

Linea leaped from the bear, ran directly at Solon Kai. He pulled to a stop and dismounted.

Odd. She was screaming at him, inches from his face.

I pushed Lump hard, but by the time I caught up, they had Linea surrounded. As I neared, the guns turned to me.

"Close enough, *Slingleston*, or we'll shoot your bears."

I dismounted in a dead run, straight for Solon Kai.

He pulled his snow knife.

And I pulled mine.

"Papa! NO!"

Linea punched straight up, hyperextending
Solon Kai's elbow. The knife flew. She brought
him down, pinned his arm as the knife stabbed
only snow.

I turned to Linea.

"Papa?"

She sighed.

"He is the tribal leader, the one I told you
about. He is my father."

"You mean . . . I—I'm dating a—a princess?"

"I would hardly call it *dating*, Wes. I mean, we
have shared a camp or two, but—"

Solon Kai protested.

"You are with this, this—city scum?"

"Hey, watch it—"

"Papa! We do not have time for this!"

She let him up. Then I noticed the silence.

"Linea, something's wrong. No planes."

"You can only run so far out here, Boy *Slinglemon*. Give in to what is inevitable."

I knew I shouldn't have left Father. I unslung the snow knife, detached the cup-hilt, refolded the strap to sit against my back. Had to prep for silent running.

"We're going back, all right, Solon Kai, all of us. But I'm not giving in."

"Wes?"

"Not yet, anyway. Linea, I need you to return with your father. I'll be along with the bears."

Lump snorted.

I circled in from a different angle. By the time I made it back, Father was surrounded by airmen and Solon Kai. Linea was there. Wilkes spoke to Father.

"When I lost my first ship, I blamed you."

"You have what you want, Wilkes. You have the City and they'll snow praises on you back home."

Wilkes chortled.

"I want it all, Singleton. For that, I need the City *and* the Device."

"You haven't a clue what it's for or how to use it."

"Neither do you, I suspect; otherwise, you would've."

"Do you realize how unique this place is? How incredible?"

"Incredible enough for me to claim it, certainly."

"You haven't suffered a tenth of what I have to find it."

"You think it was easy tracking that son of yours? He's as wily on the ice as you ever were. Maybe better. I think you're losing him to the White."

Wilkes moved to one of the airmen.

"See if Edwards has cleared the mooring mast."

"We've uh, we've lost contact with the ship, Commander."

"Get a radioman on it!"

"Aye, sir."

"I'm glad you finally figured it all out, Singleton, after listening to you prattle on about it for years. So. The Device. What's keeping your little snowdog brat?"

"My son is probably leagues away with it by now. I can't give you what I don't have."

"Of course you will. Your wife wants you to."

"You know nothing about Elizabeth."

"Oh, but I do. I know lots about her. Y'see, your raptor made it back."

Galen looked puzzled. Wilkes shouted to an airman.

"Lieutenant! Where's my radioman?"

"He's not at his post, sir, and the radio's gone."

"Find Edwards! We are LEAVING!"

Wilkes turned back to Galen.

"Don't look surprised, Singleton. I figured out your little code. 'Nowhere' becomes 'Now Here.'"

Wilkes grinned.

"Once it crossed the Boundary Lands, I sent someone to talk to Elizabeth about the scrambled coordinates."

"She wouldn't talk to just anyone, Wilkes."

"You're right, she didn't. She just needed a little—persuasion."

"Said the man about to die."

"Well, now, that's much better. The ever-protective son appears."

Father's mustache drooped.

"Wes! Wh—why did you come back?"

"That wasn't the deal, Wilkes. I get my father, you get the credit for the City."

"You're as gullible as your whole family, son."

"Wes?"

"It was the only way to get outfitted to find you, Father."

"You set up *my own son*?"

"Added bonus, Singleton. Now I can erase your whole pitiful family."

Staring at me as he was, I could fairly read the pride in Father's face as he spoke.

"Only the Singleton family would know that the quest is worth more than the prize, Wilkes. But I wouldn't expect you to understand that."

"Father—wait. . . . I'm not letting this thief have everything."

"I won't let you risk your life for this, either."

"I've *already* risked my life."

"And I couldn't be more proud. Wes, *this* is how we fail better."

"Oh bra-vo! Such thick blood between you two!"
Solon Kai yelled.
"You should give him the machine, *Singsington*!"
Father and I both shouted.
"It's SINGLETON!"
Wilkes pulled a repeater from his waistcoat.

"ENOUGH! I'll put you *both* out of my misery!"

He cocked the hammer, pointed it at Father.

"In the real world, Singleton, good guys finish last. Now . . . the Device!"

"Wes, this guy will take your *life* before he takes the Device, no questions asked."

"Father—"

"NOW, SINGLETON!"

"All right! You want the Device? Fine!"

I walked to the edge of the massive hole and pointed.

"It's down there!"

Wilkes got in my face.

"You think I survived these scars by being stupid? It's right there in your knapsack!"

"Oh, right! Well . . . been around for centuries, eh, Wilkes? What's a few more?"

"Wesley, NO!"

I tossed the pack—right into the cauldron of the Engine.

"NOW! I meant *NOW* it's down there!"

Wilkes changed his aim to me. Spoke through his teeth.

"You *idiot*! I should've left your daddy in that cave years ago! You've been a real pain in the neck, Singleton. Just like your *old man!*"

"Funny you should mention that."

A deep, primal growl filled the chamber. An airman cried out.

"Commander! Behind you!"

Grim slammed his chest. Wilkes shot backward,
windless, spun in a long silent fall.

The airmen closed around us as Father spoke.

"Lower your weapons, boys. I'm taking command of the ship."

"Hold on, Singleton."

Tomison Edwards stepped from outside the circle of airmen.

"Don't you think you'd better clear it with the next-in-command?"

"Edwards! Switched sides, have you?"

"What do you take me for, a turncoat?"

"What would you have me think?"

"*Somebody* had to keep track of that maniac, and I thought what better place than to be right under his nose?"

"Then you would've—"

"I was gonna figure that out later, once Wilkes had the blasted Device. You beat me to it, as usual, but we still haven't got it!"

Galen smiled.

"Father, Grim's condition is serious. He needs medical attention, stat!"

Edwards addressed the men.

"Right. You may stand down, gentlemen. I'm assuming command of this vessel. And we have very precious cargo. Get this beast to the infirmary!"

NEXT MORNING

Father's eyes burned, hardened and war torn, as he spoke.

"I shouldn't have risked losing the City without you, Wes."

"You're saying—"

"That we should go back together, find the Arktos Device, and claim the City for ourselves. As we always should've."

"I can't . . ."

"Wesley. *Son.* When you were a boy, I was hard on you. Neglectful."

"Without an ice crawler's doubt."

"Guess I deserve that. I was so focused on the prize, I couldn't see anything else."

"Mother included."

"You've no idea."

"Oh, I've a very clear perspective on that one, Father."

"I wanted you to fulfill your *own* passions. It had to be entirely yours."

"You had an odd way of showing me how to do that."

"It was all I knew. I was not about to lose you to—"

His voice cracked. He looked away.

"You need to get home, Father."

"I can't just leave you here."

"Well, you'll have to, because I can't go back quite yet."

Linea and I exchanged glances. Father noticed, raised an eyebrow, and spoke.

"Well, don't worry about ol' Grim here. He's lucky the first shot ricocheted off his harness buckle. Missed his lung. He just needs a little stitching up. But wait—how do you plan on getting back?"

"We've got the bears to guide us."

I couldn't resist smiling.

"I see. Well, I've some unfinished business myself, Wes."

"Sam?"

Father winked, with a twist of his head.

Sam. I knew that injury was a bite.

Father grew serious again.

"Son. I want you to know . . . I— I . . ."

It was still hard for him.

"I'll be along soon enough—Dad."

I stared out over the endless mountains.

"Looks like good guys *do* finish first, Wilkes—right after the jerks give up."

I turned to the bears.

"Whaddya say, boys . . . home to the monastery? I promise, no more bad guys to—"

They ignored me, grunted, walked ahead. Linea had an odd look on her face.

"Girls."

"Huh?"

She shook her head.

"Girls. They are all female, Wes."

"But I thought . . . and you said—"

"I doubt they believe you, either."

She smiled.

". . . but I do."

Linea headed downhill. It would take five days to get back. If lucky, three. Then, the search for the real Arcturus would begin.

And I was pretty sure Father would support that.

Maybe one *can* lose a childhood and gain a father, or an airship pilot can learn to love the ice.

Maybe . . . just maybe, the Phantom Waste is my home.

ACKNOWLEDGMENTS

I've been an artist all of my life, creating visuals for other people's ideas to make a living as an illustrator. In that world I learned to collaborate and work as part of a team to accomplish a visual goal. When it came to painting my own ideas, I was completely autonomous in the effort.

I thought writing would be the same: one person in a room, coming up with ideas, writing them down, and coming away with a completely personal view.

I found quickly that I was mistaken. Just as we are not raised in a vacuum of ideas, we do not create in a vacuum either. I discovered that in sharing my ideas with friends and colleagues, I was drawn back into the collaborative effort that I'd learned as a professional illustrator.

People love ideas. When new, they're like fresh clay, moldable and pliable, shifting from moment to moment. My artist and author friends taught me how to share ideas, take critique, and reshape those thoughts again. I realized that an idea like this book relies on the support of the people around you who want to see you succeed.

An idea like this is never accomplished alone.

First, I have to thank my long-time friend, author, and polymath **Cat Peterson** for not only the encouragement to write, but for his exclamation when he first saw my character with the bears ("Get that in front of a publisher!") His wife, **Anne Murphy**, a lover of all bears, consistently pushed for "more bears!" in the story and art. From Anne, who said, "All good writing is rewriting," which started me on my way, to Cat, who kept the pressure on throughout: thank you both. Whenever the inevitable doubt crept in, your stalwart support was enlivening.

Marcelo Anciano—a UK publisher, art director, director, screenwriter, and art collector who became a great friend and confidante—was indispensable. Our tireless, hours-long phone calls across the pond about writing and cinema proved critical to my entire process. I learned most how to listen and accept alternate notions about my story. He kept me on track, like a through line. Thanks, Marcelo, for all of your help and sharp critique.

Kim Kincaid suggested that I stay with a male lead because, as an ex-librarian, she was always trying to find books for boys to get excited about. She loved my initial ideas for the story, and it was Kim who first thought that one of my snowdogs was a girl, which gave me Linea as a character. We lost Kim in 2015, just as she was building her own beautiful series of paintings. She'll never know now how much she's meant to me and this story.

One summer night at Amherst Coffee, I was talking some friends through the story when **Holly Black** walked in and said, "Story? What story?" It's not everyday a *New York Times* bestselling author takes focused interest in your idea. She stayed up until the small hours of the morning asking questions and made me realize what I'd taken on. My work had only just begun. Thanks for the shakedown, Holly!

My thanks to many artist friends willing to help in any way: **Dave Seeley** took my drawings and built a 3-D model of the SnowTracker to help me get it right, and he put up with my many adjustments; **Tony Palumbo** turned my drawings into models of the airships and cut my drawing work by more than half; **John Hayes** skinned the Mosquitos in silver and lit them just the way I needed; and **Lars Grant-West** lent his eye to my polar bear anatomy whenever I asked—I'll likely be calling him again soon. And **Michael Kaluta** let me pick from his extensive collection of pilot gear to use! Thanks, you guys.

Big polar bear hugs and thanks to the entire O'Brien family. Tim played Galen Singleton, while his wife, Elizabeth Parisi, played Elizabeth Singleton. And especially to their son, Cassius, who was a natural for Wesley.

Thanks also to a fine bunch of illustrators affectionately called the Group, who I e-mail on regular occasions and who all offered comments and critiques for the initial fifteen paintings: **Julie Bell**, **Sam Burley**, **Dan Dos Santos**, **Scott M. Fischer**, **Donato Giancola**, **Lars Grant-West**, **Doug Alexander Gregory**, **Rebecca Guay**, **Bruce Jensen**, **Todd Lockwood**, **Stephan Martinière**, **Dave Seeley**, **Cyril Van Der Haegen**, and **Boris Vallejo**.

Many thanks to several beta readers, specifically **Geralyn Monti** and **Scott Brundage**, who helped keep it real. Their suggestions and excitement for the tale were invaluable, and **Jared Shear** for keeping my supply of canvas and brushes topped off. Thanks for the shots of snowy Montana and composition suggestions, too. And to **Scott Anderson** who texted for eleven months to check on my sanity. You guys are the Best.

There are many thousands of readers on the **Muddy Colors** blog who I shared my process with along the way. Thank you all for your abiding anticipation and encouragement to get through it.

Thanks to **all of my students** around the world who believed in my work, my teaching, and my relentless talks with them about rejecting talent for focused training. Their support and delight for the images kept me rolling.

Without my editor, **Joe Monti**, you would not be holding this book in your hands. He championed this idea from start to finish. It was a joy to work with and learn from him. Thanks, Joe. **Michael McCartney**, associate art director at Saga Press, kept the design subtle and classy and stayed open to my involvement. Thanks too, Michael. And when my agent, **Charlie Olsen**, over at InkWell Management saw this for the first time, his enthusiasm alone gave me the strength to push through. His encouragement and fostering continues to inspire me to ever bigger risks. Thanks so much.

And finally, certainly, and above all to **Irene Gallo**, who when asked what I should paint for a video about my working process said, "You like snow. What about a guy riding a polar bear or something?" From her thoughts seven years ago came not only this grand effort, but a paradigm shift in my skills and a string of new worlds to paint. Irene, I cannot thank you enough, or with more love.

To my big brother, Warren. You stirred a young boy's dreams of adventure with real-life quests by becoming a pilot, a fencer, and nearly an astronaut. When you showed me the magic held within an ordinary pencil, you ignited my life as an artist. You inspire me to this day.

SAGA PRESS
AN IMPRINT OF SIMON & SCHUSTER, INC.

1230 AVENUE OF THE AMERICAS, NEW YORK, NEW YORK 10020